‖‖‖‖‖‖‖‖‖‖‖‖‖‖‖
◁ **W9-BEI-788**

HARLEQUIN®
Presents

Welcome to the December 2008 collection of
Harlequin Presents!

This month, be sure to read Lynne Graham's
The Greek Tycoon's Disobedient Bride, the first
book in her exciting new trilogy, VIRGIN BRIDES,
ARROGANT HUSBANDS. Plus, don't miss the second
installment of Sandra Marton's THE SHEIKH TYCOONS
series, *The Sheikh's Rebellious Mistress.* Get whisked
off into a world of glamour, luxury and passion in
Abby Green's *The Mediterranean Billionaire's
Blackmail Bargain,* in which innocent Alicia finds
herself falling for hard-hearted Dante. Italian tycoon
Luca O'Hagan will stop at nothing to make Alice his
bride in Kim Lawrence's *The Italian's Secretary Bride,*
and in Helen Brooks's *Ruthless Tycoon, Innocent
Wife,* virgin Marianne Carr will do anything to save
her home, and ruthless Rafe Steed is on hand to help
her. Things begin to heat up at the office for interior
designer Merrow in Trish Wylie's *His Mistress,
His Terms,* when playboy Alex sets out to break
all the rules. Independent Cally will have one night
she'll never forget with bad-boy billionaire Blake in
Natalie Anderson's *Bought: One Night, One Marriage.*
And find out if Allie can thaw French doctor
Remy de Brizat's heart in Sara Craven's
Bride of Desire. Happy reading!

We'd love to hear what you think about Presents.
E-mail us at Presents@hmb.co.uk or join in the
discussions at www.iheartpresents.com and
www.sensationalromance.blogspot.com, where you'll
also find more information about books and authors!

kept for his
Pleasure

She's his mistress on demand!

Whether seduction takes place in his king-size bed, a five-star hotel, his office or beachside penthouse, these fabulously wealthy, charismatic and sexy men know how to keep a woman coming back for more! Commitment might not be high on his agenda—or even on it at all!

She's his mistress on demand—but when he wants her body *and* soul he will be demanding a whole lot more! Dare we say it...even marriage!

Don't miss any books in this exciting new miniseries from Harlequin Presents!

In February 2009, look out for the next one:
Confessions of a Millionaire's Mistress
by Robyn Grady

Trish Wylie

HIS MISTRESS, HIS TERMS

kept for his
Pleasure

HARLEQUIN®

TORONTO • NEW YORK • LONDON
AMSTERDAM • PARIS • SYDNEY • HAMBURG
STOCKHOLM • ATHENS • TOKYO • MILAN • MADRID
PRAGUE • WARSAW • BUDAPEST • AUCKLAND

ISBN-13: 978-0-373-12786-3
ISBN-10:   0-373-12786-3

HIS MISTRESS, HIS TERMS

First North American Publication 2008.

All about the author...
Trish Wylie

TRISH WYLIE tried various careers before becoming a writer. She flicked her blond hair over her shoulder while playing the promotions game, worked for a while in the music business, smiled sweetly at awkward customers during the retail nightmare known as the run-up to Christmas and has gotton completely lost in her car in every single town in Ireland while working as a sales rep. It took all that character-building and a healthy sense of humor to get her dream job, she feels. Now she spends her days in reindeer slippers, with her hair in whatever band she can find to keep it out of the way and makeup as vague and distant a memory as manicured nails, while she gets to create the kind of dream man she'd still like to believe is out there somewhere. If it turns out he is, she promises she'll let you know...after she's been out for a new wardrobe, a manicure and a makeover....

To my blog readers—who helped sprinkle the fairy dust with their enthusiasm for this story. You *all* rock!

CHAPTER ONE

'MERROW O'CONNELL?'

What the hell kind of a name was that anyway? Alex exhaled on a huff of air; he had better things to do with his time than traipse halfway across Dublin in search of the damn elusive woman with the ridiculous name. And it wasn't as if his patience wasn't already sorely pushed to the limit these days by the demands of a certain client! But then if it weren't for that client he wouldn't *be* traipsing in the first place, would he?

He could remember his life being simpler. Not that long ago as it happened. It just *felt* longer…

'Up here.'

The female voice he recognised from the phone sounded from above, so he took a step back and tilted his chin up to try and see where it had come from. At the top of some scaffolding, flat on her back while applying gold leaf to an intricate Moroccan pattern on the ceiling, was his prey. And prey she was, make no mistake—he was getting her for this project if he had to make a deal with the devil.

He wanted the simpler version of his life back.

'I spoke to you on the phone earlier.'

'That must have been a treat for you. I'm famous for my sexy phone voice.'

Her voice *had* been sexy on the phone; at least he'd thought so at the time. Well, he'd thought it until she'd cut him short and hung up on him. People in this city did *not* hang up on a Fitzgerald. It was practically unheard of if they planned on having a successful career. And it had left him staring angrily at the phone for a good ten minutes before he decided to take the bull by the horns.

'You said you were too busy to come to the office so I decided to come see you in per—'

'And as you can see, I'm *still busy.* I don't see how anything barring an organ transplant couldn't have waited 'til tomorrow, Mr Fitzgerald.'

A wise ass, great, exactly what he needed about now. 'Ordinarily I'd agree with you, but my client is persistent, and if I don't nail down an interior designer soon the whole project will fall behind…'

Well, it wasn't *entirely* a lie… He just left out the part where, if he didn't get an interior designer soon, he would probably be up on the charge of *murdering* his client. Even if it was technically 'self-defence'—the very fact he'd contemplated it made it premeditated.

'Another day wouldn't have mattered. I'll be done with this by then.'

He watched as her long fingers gently pushed the last of the gold leaf into place with some kind of applicator. 'Well, I'm here now. Is there any chance you might come down here for five minutes before you start another sheet?'

'There is if you ask nicely.'

He took a steadying breath, forcing the word through tight lips. 'Please?'

'*Pretty* please?'

Alex swore underneath his breath and heard soft, musical

laughter from above. If she hadn't been the one designer his client was hell-bent on getting then he'd have told her exactly where she could put 'pretty please' about now…

'All right, I'm coming down.'

He took a step back, glancing around the room as she made her way down the scaffolding. An interesting, if somewhat opulent design for a restaurant in his opinion, but hey, whatever the client wanted, right? The mosaic tiling on the floor must have been a right cow to put down though…so maybe she knew how to work with difficult clients already?

When two dusty work boots appeared in his line of vision his gaze slowly raised, over equally dusty denim dungarees at least two sizes too big for the frame beneath them, until he was looking at her face.

Alex gaped openly. And Alex *never* gaped. He'd been brought up better than that.

Her green eyes widened. *'You?'*

'You're Merrow O'Connell?'

'And *you're* Alexander Fitzgerald?' A wide smile spread across her lush lips. 'Well, well, isn't *this* interesting?'

He shoved his fisted hands into his trouser pockets and rewarded her smile with a frown, determined not to smile back even though he could feel a smile forming in his chest. But she'd reeled him in with a smile last time, hadn't she?

'You can't be Merrow O'Connell.' Not that she'd been keen to *provide* a name last time… 'Red' he had called her in the end.

Merrow folded her arms across the front of her dungarees and tilted her head, a long loose strand of wavy auburn hair dangling across her throat. 'And why can't I?'

'Because I'm not spending the next nine months working with you after—'

'One night of incredibly hot uncomplicated sex?'

When she accompanied the question with a knowing sparkle in her eyes, he pressed his mouth into a thin line. He didn't need this, really he didn't. He must have been so-o-o bad in a previous life.

But he was an adult, he could handle awkward situations, so he had such a problem with this because…?

Well, because the millisecond he'd realised who it was he was talking to his mind had remembered every single second of that one night, vividly. And judging by the rush of blood southwards from his brain his body would have no problem with a repeat performance. An all-night repeat performance, slow and hot, possibly with different accessories—not that the silk scarf hadn't worked for him just fine last time, but maybe something more velvety, or feathers, or—

See, this was *exactly* what he was worried about.

How in hell was he supposed to concentrate on *work* if he had *this* to deal with every day? She'd distract the heck out of him! And he had enough to deal with.

'And anyway,' she lifted her delicate chin and informed him haughtily, 'I haven't said I'd work with you yet. Are you always this presumptuous? Is the famous Fitzgerald name supposed to be enough to persuade me on its own? I should be on my knees in front of you about now, I suppose…'

She was babbling, but Alex's imagination did *all* kinds of things with *that* image! He closed his eyes briefly, took a breath, and then turned his head to look at her from the corners of narrowed eyes. 'Are you making fun of me now?'

'Me?' The smile teased her mouth again, 'O-o-ooh, as if I'd dare.'

He was still trying to figure out if that was another dig as she unfolded her arms and walked past him. 'I told you on the phone I'd have to see the project before I agreed to anything.'

'You said you had a *short* window in your schedule. And you won't turn it down when you see it.'

'You don't know I won't.'

'Yes, I do, 'cos any designer who loves what they do would be seriously turned on by a project this size.'

Great choice of words, Alex.

When she looked over her shoulder her eyes were sparkling with mischief again. 'Didn't anyone ever tell you size doesn't matter?'

Alex pursed his lips again and looked at the ceiling when she turned away, taking a deep breath to try and get his brain enough oxygen to work properly. Men at the grand age of thirty weren't supposed to be so close to having high blood pressure, were they?

'Well, how about you try looking at it before you make your mind up? My client is very keen on your work.' He frowned at the ceiling. She needn't think she was adding mad Moroccan influences to the beautiful lines he'd spent months designing for the Pavenham. Sure as hell not when it had taken eight drafts to get it past Mickey D and his pals.

'The Pavenham could be the kind of project to launch you into the big time…'

With a flask in her hand, Merrow turned. She blew a puff of air at the loose strand of hair before fixing her green gaze directly on his eyes. 'The Pavenham Hotel? The one that Apocalypse just bought?'

'That's the one.' He genuinely smiled this time, because he'd known she'd at least be impressed *by that*. After all, the project was already making news all over the world. 'And they have deep pockets. You'd be very well paid for your work.'

'Chamomile tea?' She held up the flask.

Alex shook his head. 'Hell, no.'

And she smiled again, damn her. That small, mischievous imp of a smile that might look cute on her when she was wearing dusty dungarees, but when she'd been wearing barely visible white shorts and a black single-button jacket that looked distinctly as if she wasn't wearing a bra underneath it…well, it'd translated differently then. It was one of the very first things that had drawn him to her that unusually sultry September night in Galway. She had smiled that smile and Alex's body had leapt to attention. Literally.

Even the memory of it now was doing the same thing all over again.

Her voice dropped to a seductive edge. 'It might help you with all that tension.'

He frowned again, removing his hands from his pockets to fold his arms across his broad chest. 'What tension?'

'Mickey D must be giving you hell.'

Oh, *that* tension. Alex tilted his head in challenge. 'You think I can't handle an ageing rocker like Mickey D?'

'I think you wouldn't have chased halfway across Dublin looking for me if he wasn't digging his heels in. He's famous for being a bit of a prima donna…' She tilted her head at a similar angle to his and smiled another mischievous imp of a smile. 'I was conceived to one of his songs, you know.'

'Actually, I'm not sure I needed to know that. But I'm sure he'll love it when you tell him.'

She waved the flask back and forth. 'Seriously, chamomile is great stuff—and completely natural.'

'I'm good, thanks.'

Merrow shrugged, and when she focussed on unscrewing the flask's cap, pouring light golden liquid into it, he used the time to study what she was wearing. Honestly? He mightn't have paid so much attention to her the first time round if she'd been wearing that get-up. But knowing as well as he did what the loose material was hiding meant for the first time in his life, denim dungarees held a certain amount of attraction.

Underneath that denim and the madly coloured lime-green and purple sweater she curved in all the places Alex had always thought a woman should curve. She'd smelled vaguely of lavender, had amazingly soft skin, pert, tight little breasts that just spilled out of his large hands, long legs that wrapped around his waist while he…

Alex swallowed hard. And she'd *had* underwear as it turned out; tiny lace scraps straight out of any red-blooded male fantasies…which made him wonder what she was wearing now…

'So what happened to your last interior designer?'

'Which one?'

He watched as a finely arched eyebrow rose, as her mouth formed a perfect 'o' to blow over the rim of the lid before she blinked her long lashes at him and asked, 'How many have there been?'

'Four.' Which was still four less than the number of times he'd done the architectural designs but, even so… 'Mickey D is quite particular.'

'So I'm a last resort, am I?'

'Actually you're the first one that he's been determined he has to have.'

She took a sip of tea and laughed softly as she walked past him. 'Mmm. I doubt I'm really *the first*.'

Somehow the thought of some guy like Mickey D wanting more than Merrow's design skills didn't sit well with Alex. And the fact that it didn't sit well bugged him. It was none of his bloody business. Didn't stop his terse answer though.

'That kind of recruiting he can do on his own. I'm his architect, not his pimp.'

Merrow's eyebrows both rose. 'Seriously, there's more tea in the flask.'

Dammit! It could have been any other woman on the planet and Alex would have been *much* happier.

He unfolded his arms and put his hands back into his pockets, fully aware of the fact he was fidgeting. And Alex didn't fidget. That was another thing he'd been taught not to do. 'Why don't you just look at the place and see what you think?'

He tacked on something extra for good measure. 'Please.'

'Well, please certainly helps, though if you'd waited twenty-four hours I'd have gone to see it anyway. It's what I'd planned on doing...'

'You could have said that *on the phone.*'

'Thought I had—' she shrugged '—but, in fairness, when you rang I was having a goldfish crisis. I did tell you to call me back tomorrow.'

Alex stared at her for a long, long time.

Until eventually Merrow couldn't take the silence any more. 'What?'

He shook his head.

And Merrow felt another bubble of laughter working its way up from her chest. This was just too, too surreal. Mr-Best-Sex-Of-Her-Life was Alexander *Fitzgerald*? Who knew? Not that knowing would probably have stopped her from going for it that night. He was the sexiest guy she'd ever laid eyes on—had been able to turn her on with a glance—had brought her body to that humming-all-over-afterwards point that few women got to experience. And how many times in a sensible girl's life did she have an opportunity for one night of abandon? Men might have no problem with the whole one-night-stand thing, but women—well, Irish women at least—still had a little catching up to do.

Merrow felt that one fantasy night was her doing her part for feminism…and a great deal for her own sense of sexual empowerment. Her mother would have been *so* proud…

She sipped her tea and waited for him to say something. Anything. He could have read out the football scores and she'd have listened. He had a great voice; a deep, rumbling voice. No wonder she'd felt a tingle run up her spine when he'd spoken to her on the phone. She just hadn't put the two voices together into the same person in her mind—after all, it *had* been several months ago.

Her mysterious Galway guy had been relaxed, casually dressed, totally at ease, funny as hell and sexy as sin. Alexander Fitzgerald from Fitzgerald & Son the architects had been brusque and impatient on the phone, and in the flesh was dressed all city-business-guy uptight. Though the sexy as sin was still there…

Kinda made her think about loosening him up some.

His hazel eyes narrowed slightly, and he pursed his lips together so that the dimple in the centre of his chin deepened. Then his square jaw rose, light from the windows shining off the short spikes of blond hair as he asked her in a deep grumble, 'Are you this difficult to work with too?'

'I wasn't aware I was being difficult.' She blinked innocently and sipped her tea.

'Can you do tomorrow morning at nine?'

'We-ell, I'd have to check my busy schedule—' She grinned when his mouth narrowed again. He was so-o-o easy to wind up! And the Pavenham Hotel was a hu-uge project; the kind of project a career could indeed be built on. It was almost enough to make her mouth water more than the initial sight of Alex in Galway had. *Almost.* But for different reasons obviously.

'I can do nine.'

'Good.' His broad shoulders dropped the tiniest amount, his thick dark blond lashes flickering as he studied her eyes. 'I assume you know where it is?'

'Big old wreck of a mausoleum on Aston Quay?'

'That's the one.'

'Then, yes, I do know where it is.' She sipped tea and waited. Because judging by the way he'd just shifted his weight from one foot to the other there was more to come. He really should try some tea. Or a Valium. Or the only other thing she could think of to relieve all that tension...

Okay, and now the room was warm. 'Is there more?'

'Is the fact we slept together going to be an issue if we work together?'

She couldn't resist. 'I don't remember much sleeping.'

His voice dropped into a professional tone. 'This project is worth—'

'Millions. Mmm, you mentioned that on the phone.' She nodded, her eyes still staring up at him. 'So?'

'I was going to say it's worth a lot to me.'

'Why? What makes it more special than any other project Fitzgerald & Son has ever worked on before?'

He frowned, and avoided her direct gaze. 'That doesn't matter—'

'Apparently it does.'

'I won't have the project messed up—'

'Well, then, maybe it would be better if I just didn't turn up tomorrow at nine? Since you have such faith in my abilities...' Her chin rose in challenge. *Ha!*

She marched past him to replace the lid onto the flask. 'Now, if you'll excuse me, I have work to do.'

A list of horrible names for the new version of him was forming in her mind when his voice sounded again; lower this time, with an edge of resignation. 'Look. It's like this: Mickey D and his Apocalypse friends are making me crazy—have been for six months. They're *difficult*. I don't need the added hassle of working with someone else who's that difficult on a daily basis—it's already complicated enough.'

'You don't know anything about me, *Alexander*.'

'It's Alex, as *you* well know.' She heard him turn, felt the air behind her displace as he leaned his head closer to her to speak in a husky voice close by her ear, just as he had when he'd once used words to seduce her. 'And therein lies the problem, *Merrow*. 'Cos I *know* more about you than I've ever known about any other woman I've worked with before. And *that* can't get in the way.'

Merrow swallowed hard and willed her pulse to calm down. 'What you need is someone who can work *with* you on the project. Not *against* you.'

'*Exactly*.'

She felt his breathing stirring the hair against the nape of her neck, felt her own breathing speed up, her voice dropping. 'Someone who can design the interior without taking away from the architecture.'

'Precisely.'

When she turned her head his gaze shifted from the top of her head as if he'd just been caught doing something he shouldn't have. Or more likely been caught doing something he didn't want to be doing. Ha again! He wasn't any more immune to the original spark of chemistry between them than she was, was he? Well, *this time* she knew who she was dealing with. And she wasn't so sure she liked this version of him enough to go down that road again, *so there!*

She ran her tongue over her lips, watched as his gaze dropped, so with a mischievous smile she bit down on her lower lip, which made him frown. And when he looked into her eyes she tilted her head to one side, studying the gold flecks in the hazel for a second before she continued.

'What you want is a designer that can be guided artistically by you, one that's *malleable*...'

She let her tongue linger on the word 'malleable' and watched the gold in his eyes spark dangerously. But before he could say anything she reached up to straighten his tie, tightening it overly firmly around his neck as her eyes focussed on the task. 'I'll be there tomorrow, *Alex*—to meet your client—because he *wants me*. But I won't be moulded by anyone.'

She patted the tie with the palm of one hand, vaguely noting how tight his chest was beneath his shirt before she took a step backwards and looked up into his hooded eyes. 'Not even by someone I know is so *very good* with his hands...'

Alex practically growled at her.

'Now I have gold leaf to smooth into place. Which takes a high level of concentration and a fine touch.' She smiled sweetly. 'So you'll have to excuse me.'

'Merrow—'

But she ignored the warning tone in his voice, turning to set her foot onto the scaffolding. 'Bye-bye, Alex. I'll see you in the morning.'

She was halfway up the scaffolding before she heard his mumbled words on the way out the door. 'Well, that's more than you managed last time.'

Flat on her back again she stared up at the ceiling, but she didn't even attempt to lift another sheet of the delicate gold leaf. Instead she dug her mobile out of her pocket and hit Lisa's number.

'Hi, it's me. Remember Lou's hen weekend at the Oyster Festival in Galway?'

'When you met Mr-Über-Hot?'

'Yep. Well, remember we swore what happened in Galway would stay in Galway?'

'Yuh-huh.'

'I've run into a bit of a problem with that…'

CHAPTER TWO

AND you have to wear the green nineteen-twenties dress—it's gorgeous on you!

Merrow smoothed her palms down over the front of the dress, glad she'd been talked into it. If clothes made the man then they boosted the woman's confidence no end. It was a law of nature.

Hair down. No, up in something chic. No, definitely down—men love long hair.

Like she cared what Alex Fitzgerald loved! But down had won, mainly because it was easier. On one of her usual whims she tied a long silk scarf of the same deep shimmering olive green over her head like a wide Alice band, the ends flowing down her back beneath her hair.

And heels, you have to have heels on. How tall is he? Yum! Okay, then, definitely heels...

The heels maybe hadn't been the best plan in the world, especially when she decided she needed coffee from the far side of the bridge at the bottom of O'Connell Street. Because when she had to queue to get her extra large cinnamon latte it meant she had to run back over the bridge to get to the Pavenham for bang on nine—and running in heels while carrying said extra large coffee without ending up wearing it was no easy trick. She even laughed at the ridiculousness of it along the way. But the fact was, getting wardrobe advice from her friends over numerous cocktails the night before meant that coffee was a necessity…

It would serve Alex damn Fitzgerald right if she'd turned up in her work dungarees again. After all, this was work, it wasn't a *date!*

Which didn't really explain why her pulse hiccupped at the sight of him standing outside the old hotel, but then, in fairness, he did look *hot*. And much more like the Galway Alex she remembered now he was out of a suit again. Instead he had on comfy-looking blue jeans and a crisp white shirt, worn loose, unbuttoned at the neck, with rolled up sleeves.

The sun came out from behind a cloud and glinted on his blond hair. So Merrow glanced heavenwards, shaking her head. 'Not helping.'

He adjusted the camera strap he had draped off one shoulder, pacing up and down as he spoke on the phone, his movements fluid, hinting at physical strength and confidence. Mind you, if Merrow had been born a boy and ended up looking like that she'd have been confident too. Add to his looks the fact that she now knew he came from one of the richest, oldest, best-known families in the country and, well…the fact that he was gorgeous as well seemed a tad unfair to the rest of mankind…

Just as well he had a tendency towards acting like a bit of an ass, really. It was a karmic balance thing, wasn't it?

As she thought that very thought he laughed out loud in response to whatever his phone friend said. And even through the sounds of traffic and people she could hear it: the deep, oh-so-male sound dancing through the background noise and translating straight into an answering smile on her face. Well, hell. It wasn't as if he was laughing for *her* benefit!

A random person in the crowd bumped her shoulder, causing her to hold her coffee out so she wouldn't end up cinnamon-scented having got safely all the way across the bridge. So, with a smaller smile at the rushed apology, she focussed her attention on dodging the traffic to get to Alex's side of the road.

He flipped his phone shut, pushing it into the back pocket of his jeans as she approached, any hint of laughter gone from his face as he studied her from top to toe with hooded eyes.

'Good morning!' She pinned a hundred-watt smile on her face. 'Not waiting long, I hope?'

Alex glanced at his watch. 'Nope, you're bang on time. Not that I can say the same thing about Mickey.'

'Rock stars can't be on time; it's too conventional for them.'

'Hmm.' He gave her a sideways glance that translated to Merrow as his believing she'd understand unconventional better than he would, which, in fairness, was probably true. But even so…

She tilted her head. '*So*, do you want to walk me through your plans while we wait or shall we stand out here and discuss the weather?'

'Maybe we should talk about yesterday first.'

'Or maybe we should try to go one itty-bitty day without annoying each other or ending up horizontal?'

Accompanying the question with another smile didn't stop Alex frowning. 'You see, that's exactly what we need to talk about. You can't talk to me like that in front of a client, or the building crew.'

'And you can't talk to me in the patronising tone you'd use on a twelve-year-old and not expect me to retaliate.' She blew into the tiny hole in the top of her coffee-cup. 'I know how to behave around clients. And building crews like a bit of banter, especially from a girl; they work harder to impress her that way. If you can't have a bit of craic at work from time to time then the days can get *lo-ong*.'

When she glanced up at him from beneath her long lashes he was staring at her with a stony-faced expression. 'And I remember you having more of a sense of humour before. Did you rent it from somewhere for your weekend in Galway?'

'Do you bait me on purpose?'

'Nope, but it seems to be a talent, doesn't it? Maybe if you didn't take yourself so seriously it wouldn't be so *easy...*'

'I take *my work* seriously.'

'And so you should, but not to the point of stuffiness—a little charm can work wonders.'

'You think I can't be charming?' The gold in his eyes sparkled. 'Now, Merrow, you know better than that.'

And there it was. That hint of a smile that, when accompanied with the sparkle in his eyes, made every bit of her itch to tease the smile out properly. He'd done that in Galway too. She just needed to remember what it was she'd done then to make it happen... Mmm...

Her forefinger tapped absent-mindedly against her coffee-cup while she thought. She was fairly sure *that* was illegal at nine o'clock in the morning, in public, while standing beside the Liffey. Tempting though...

Just remember he's being an ass.

He glanced down at her high heels with a thoughtful expression on his face, then his gaze rose, slowly, studying every inch of her exposed calves, until he looked up at her face from beneath his lashes, and stepped closer. 'I can be charming. I can be *more* than charming if it gets me the results I want.'

Uh-oh. This was a new tactic. Now, you see, him being an ass she could work with; him being charming, well, *more* than charming—that she might have to think some about. It would actually be simpler if he stayed an ass. And she could help with that.

So she lifted her chin and looked down her nose at him. 'I've no evidence of that in *business*—' she shrugged one shoulder '—and I don't mix business with pleasure, Mr Fitzgerald. I take my job *very* seriously.'

Then she lifted her cup, took a sip and smiled.

After a brief moment of silence Alex stunned her by laughing, the sound even more affecting physically up close than it had been from across the street. '*Touché*, Miss O'Connell. There's never going to be a dull moment with you around, is there?'

Merrow turned slightly on one heel and looked up and down the street, studying random faces. 'I'm sorry, are *all* of your multiple personalities here? If I'd known, I'd have said hello to all of them…'

Long, warm fingers circled her elbow, pulling her towards the large oak doors. 'Come on. Let's go look inside. And if you manage to get Mickey D off my case I'll think about being charming more often.'

'Is that a threat?'

He laughed again, shaking his head as he pulled open the door. 'It's a promise—a heartfelt one.'

Once inside he stepped back, releasing her elbow as he watched her reaction from the corner of his eye. And he told himself it was important she liked what he was doing with the hotel because he needed her to work on its interior, not because he felt the need to have his ego stroked.

Damn, but she was pretty.

When he'd seen her running over the bridge she'd taken his breath away. With her green nineteen-twenties 'flapper girl' dress and that suggestive scarf floating out behind her, she'd been a vivid splash of colour in a cityscape of grey. He hadn't expected the smile of anticipation the sight of her had brought to his face.

And he wasn't kidding. If she managed to unsettle and ruffle Mickey D the way she did him, then this might just work. She'd be due more than a little gratitude for that. He'd be *very* appreciative.

Then he'd have a reason to act out on some of the dreams he'd had the night before…some based on things they'd already done…some he'd be fully prepared to give a try, according to his body's immediate reaction every time she was around.

'Wow.'

He smiled at her expression. 'I'm glad you like it. I was just on the phone with the contractor and he informs me we're a little ahead with the renovation. So it's ready for an interior designer to step in.'

'It's huge!'

Music to any man's ears…

Alex silently cleared his throat. 'Fifty rooms, four suites and a penthouse. And a restaurant, a bar, a spa, conference rooms…you know, just enough to keep a designer out of mischief…'

She turned her head and focussed wide green eyes on him. And for the first time he saw a crack in her usual confidence; if anything she paled a little. 'Ready by *when* exactly?'

'Yesterday.'

Alex's chin dropped, he closed his eyes briefly, sighed, and opened his eyes long enough to glance apologetically at Merrow before he turned round and swept an arm out to his side. 'Merrow O'Connell, meet Mickey D—new owner of the Pavenham.'

Merrow stepped forwards, extending one fine-boned hand to

the leather-clad, sunglasses-wearing Mickey. She even cocked her hip towards him. 'Well, hello, it's lovely to finally meet you.'

Mickey took her hand and used the other to tilt his sunglasses further down his nose before he took much longer than necessary to look Merrow over. 'Well, aren't you just the prettiest thing in this place since we started? You single, Merrow O'Connell?'

She giggled. Actually giggled. Like a star-struck teenager. And Alex scowled at her back before he stepped closer to her side. 'Whether or not she's single doesn't really have any relevance to—'

'Oh, I'm terminally single. More time for my work.'

Mickey smiled a smile that showed off his gold front tooth to good effect. 'All work and no play, Merrow…'

'Oh, don't worry, Mickey.' She patted the back of the hand holding hers with her other hand, her eyes sparkling. 'I find time to play too—'

She tilted her head towards Alex, turned her face, and looked up at him with heavy-lidded eyes. 'Don't I, Alex?'

Hadn't she said she knew how to behave around clients? Well, if that was her idea of behaving then they needed to have another little chat about—

But she'd already moved on. 'Did Alex tell you I was conceived to one of your albums? My mum is a huge fan!'

Mickey let go of her hand, his smile changing a little, in tone if not in width. 'You'll have to bring her to the hotel when we're all finished up.'

'She'd *love* that.' Merrow flicked her deep auburn hair off one shoulder and leaned in closer to bat her eyelashes at him. 'Do you want to give me the grand tour in person?'

In front of Alex's amazed eyes, Mickey D—the guy who had made his life hell for months—gallantly held out a crooked elbow, grinning at Merrow as she accepted it and fitted in against his side. 'I'd love to, little lady. Love to. Have to say: love your work. I was in the nightclub you worked on in Cork—the one with the round sofa-bed things and the harem theme. Very sexy…'

Merrow winked at Alex on the way past, and handed him her coffee as if he were her assistant.

'Actually, Mickey, I've some ideas about hotels already. I read about adult hotels online; have you heard about them?'

Alex scowled. He wasn't sure if he admired the fact she'd just 'managed' his difficult client, or if he was mad at her for trying to turn the place into some kind of twenty-first century brothel underneath his nose, or if he was just plain furious that she'd pressed her body so close into Mickey's side.

While he tried to figure it out, he lifted the cup to his mouth without thinking, grimacing at the lid in disgust when he tasted the contents. What was *that* supposed to be?

He set it on the floor by the door.

'Alex, walk with us.' She used her 'famous sexy phone voice' from across the cavernous foyer. 'You can tell me what you've done at the same time so I have the whole picture.'

Well, it was certainly nice to be *included*. But she needn't think he was any more ready to be 'managed' than she was to be 'moulded'. This was his gig; from start to finish. His reputation depended on it. Alex was getting the '& Son' removed from the gold plaque outside the office in Merrion Square by the end of the year if it killed him. He had a *goal*.

'We'd agreed to try and incorporate a lot of Irish influences—'

'That's a great idea! How clever of you to think of it, Mickey. You're thinking natural—rough carved wood, slate, that kind of thing?'

Mickey had taken three sessions before he'd agreed to *Alex's plan*. Thanks anyway.

He stepped in front of them and pushed his hands into his jeans pockets, fixing her with a direct gaze that said he meant business. 'A lot of original cornices were saved—' he pursed his lips as she studied the roof '—and the staircase is all original. What we want is a blend of old and new.'

'I can tell you're a visionary Mickey.'

'I like to think I've a finger on the pulse of things, though Alex *has* had the odd good idea along the way. Even talked me outta some of the more outlandish ones—which is no easy thing.'

The 'odd' good idea? All right, so it was the first compliment Mickey had actually paid him without a grunt and a shrug of his shoulders, but the outlandish ideas had taken *a lot* to get out of. If Merrow had any idea just what he'd dealt with to get the project to this stage—the *monumental* amount of patience involved...

'So tell me about adult hotels, Merrow—I like the sound of them. They sound like they involve sex.'

Merrow beamed. 'Sex sells, Mickey.'

'Goddamn right it does.'

Alex was going to strangle her. 'Except there are certain *laws* to consider.'

Merrow fixed her sparkling green gaze on his face, the mischievous smile back on her full lips. 'You have a *very* dirty mind, Alex.'

Down, boy. If he had no control over anything else in this room, his body was gonna listen! His eyes narrowed in warning.

But Merrow simply tutted at him and took her hand off Mickey's arm to wander around the room, her face animated, her voice low and huskily sexy. 'Seduction. That's what I think this place should be all about. Subtle seduction—quiet, low-lit corners, textures—suedes and velvets and leather and silks offset by rough carved wood and slate underfoot and heavy tables and chairs—the masculine and the feminine.'

Alex moved over a step so he was beside Mickey as the man removed his sunglasses. And they both watched as Merrow smiled a secretive smile, closed her eyes, bit down on her bottom lip, taking a deep breath that lifted her pert breasts before she continued, 'And scents.' She sighed blissfully. 'There should be scents; fresh pine from little trees in pots, so that you get the scent as you walk past them. And then flowers—honeysuckle, roses, lavender—out of season so it hints at the luxury. So without realising it you'll associate those scents with being here. So even when you leave, months afterwards, you'll remember being here and suddenly realise you were seduced and just didn't know it at the time…'

Alex felt his body go hard. He swallowed, determined to remove the memory of *lavender scent* from his mind. He then glanced sideways at Mickey, scowling at the mesmerised expression on the older man's face.

Oh, *the hell* he was going to look at her like that while Alex stood beside him. If he even thought of laying a pinkie on her—

He looked directly at Merrow as she opened her eyes, a scowl of warning aimed in her direction as she walked slowly towards him, her gaze fixed on his as she damped her lips again.

'The Pavenham should be classic mixed with traditional mixed with modern day. It should stand out of the crowd. And its interior should feel so sensual that its visitors will want to reach out and touch things without knowing they're doing it. They should brush their fingertips over the suede—should sink lower into the velvet of the sofas—should feel a certain eroticism from the softest leathers against their skin…'

She tilted her head to one side and swayed her shoulders a little. 'When they eat in the restaurant the plainest food should taste better than anything ever has before, the wines should be richer, crisper; glasses should be heavy in their hands. There should be candles everywhere and splashes of deep, earthy colours to draw the eye and warm the soul.'

She stopped in front of them both, quirked her brows, damped her lips again with the tempting tip of her tongue and sighed. 'The Pavenham should be seduction in the city.'

After a moment's silence she tore her gaze from Alex's and smiled at Mickey D. 'Don't you think?'

Mickey remained silent for another long moment before nudging Alex hard. 'Hire her. *Now.* Give her whatever she needs.'

Merrow grinned. 'Excellent!' Then she clapped her hands together just the one time and lifted her chin to look at Alex. 'I'll run some sketches off and put together a collage and you can call me tomorrow some time if you have anything you want to talk about.'

She patted Mickey's upper arm. 'Lovely to meet you, Mickey. I'm sure I'll see you again soon. Now, where did I leave my coffee?'

Alex ground the answer out from between his clenched teeth. 'By the door.'

'Great. Bye, then!'

Alex watched her sashay all the way to the door; he watched her skirt lift when she bent over to lift her coffee, affording him a tempting view of a little more long, shapely leg. And he watched as she shouldered her way out the door with a smile on her face.

What had just happened? It felt vaguely as if he'd been run over by a bus.

'Well, she's a firecracker.' Mickey slapped him so hard on

the back that Alex rocked forward onto the balls of his feet, scowling harder.

'You have your hands full with that one.'

'Indeed.' He discovered he had a gift for understatement.

'Yup, I'm gonna look like a pussycat after working with her.' He set his sunglasses back on his nose. 'But if she can pull off even half of what she just described, then we're about to make one helluva splash here.'

'It'll work. I'll see to that.'

'Never doubted it for a second, Alex.' Mickey grinned broadly. 'You Fitzgeralds are s'posed to be the best. And I only ever pay for the best.'

No pressure there, then. But as he walked to the door with his suddenly placated client, Alex knew one thing for certain. He'd be calling Merrow all right, because there was plenty to 'talk about'. And this time *he* was going to talk, and *she* would damn well listen!

No matter *what* he had to do to get her attention...

CHAPTER THREE

'WHY are you seeing him outside of working hours? Remind me again.'

Merrow pinned the phone between her ear and her shoulder and attempted to get her leather artist portfolio into a more comfortable carrying position. 'Because he wanted to meet up and it's the only time I've got to see him. There's *nothing* going on. I told you that already.'

'Not convincingly enough, hon…'

Obviously. Because her three best friends had been what felt like *constantly* on the phone or texting. Merrow had even wondered briefly if they had some kind of tag-team going…

They were interested was all; they cared about her the same way she cared about them. That was what friends did. It was just that, after Dylan, whom an American friend had dubbed 'the schmuck', they were a little more interested in any guy Merrow might date. They were 'looking out for her'. But it was getting tiring.

Merrow took a deep breath, glancing around as she turned in a circle, trying to work out which side of Merrion Square Alex's office was on. Her eyes caught sight of the statue of Oscar Wilde leaning on a rock beyond the green railings and she silently asked him with a quirked eyebrow if he could kindly point her in the right direction…

Oscar remained silent.

'It's work.'

'It's half past seven. Work stopped at half five.'

Not necessarily. Merrow pouted her lower lip out as she wandered along the railing. 'This won't be the first work meeting I've had out of hours. People have busy lives. And speaking of which, if you don't get off the phone soon I'll be late meeting you at Temple Bar.'

'Half nine, yeah?'

'Yes. Half nine.'

'Well, if you're late, we'll understand why.'

'I won't be late.'

'If he's half as hot as I remember him being at the Oyster Festival we'll *understand*. But we'll need *all* the gory details…'

Merrow caught sight of a gold plaque on the other side of the street that looked promising. 'I *won't* be late. It's work!'

Hence why she was at his office after hours and not meeting him where he lived. There was one night of fantasy and then there was real life. And Merrow *knew* the difference between the two. *Most of the time.*

'Have fun.'

She walked across the street, readjusted her portfolio again and sighed in relief as she read the gold plate. 'Ha, ha. I'll see you in a while. Bye.'

With her phone tucked back into her bag, the strap of the bag lugged back onto her shoulder and her portfolio once again adjusted, she rang the bell on one side of the Georgian doorway. Then she smoothed her hands over her braids, checked the two loose strands of hair still framed her face, readjusted all of her baggage when it slipped again—and just about managed to have enough time to fold her arms and look calm before the door opened and Alex filled the space; *filled* being the operative word.

Oh, that was so not fair.

If he could just *once* not look so *damn* hot! Seriously. Was there a single article of clothing he didn't look good in? Or better out of, that her memory recalled. It really wasn't playing fair.

He leaned against the door jamb, the dark material of his shirt stretching across his broad chest as he pushed the red door a little wider. 'Hi.'

He could even make 'hi' sound sexy.

Her gaze moved up over his wide chest, up the broad column of his neck, past the dimple in his chin, the sensuous curve of the mouth she knew could do such wondrous things until she followed the straight line of his nose to look into his eyes.

Where the gold flecks glowed.

So she swallowed and pinned a bright smile on her face. 'I have the sketches and the collages for you.'

She held the portfolio out in front of her, which caused her bag to slip off her shoulder, so she had to take a second to adjust it. And when he didn't take the portfolio from her, it meant she had to juggle again, which irritated her no end.

'Come on up.' He pushed his shoulder off the door jamb and swung one long arm out to his side in invitation. 'My apartment is on the top floor. We can look them over there.'

His apartment? Aw, no. Hang on. This was *work!*

'Your office will do fine.'

He didn't so much as flinch, his gaze cool and steady despite the glowing gold, as he glanced over her nineteen-sixties plaid mini-dress, once again lingering longer than required on her legs. He was a bit of a legs man, wasn't he?

And Merrow had a sudden vivid memory of her legs spread wide, with the coarser hair of Alex's legs rubbing against her smooth skin. Boy-oh-boy—was it warmer than usual for this time of year or was it just her?

'Everything is locked up for the night. And I've just made something to eat. Come on up. We'll look at your sketches there.'

Protesting would have made her look immature, or, worse still, *worried*, so she lifted her chin for good measure and walked past him, waiting in the hallway until he closed the door and strode past her. So she had a great view of his tight rear on the way up the stairs…

He really did fill out a pair of jeans, didn't he?

'You live here as well? That's dedication.'

His deep voice echoed off the walls of the seemingly never-ending stairway with its intricate wrought-iron railing. 'One of my father's projects. He didn't like to be far away from his work.'

Ah, the famous Arthur Fitzgerald—a safer topic to think about. Now there was a legacy to live up to. Merrow couldn't help but think that, given the choice, she'd have chosen a different career herself. It would've been easier than living under that kind of a shadow her whole life.

She wondered if Alex ever felt that way. Somehow she doubted he was the kind of guy who would ever make that big a confession out loud.

'Bet there's a nice view from up there though.' She sighed in appreciation of her *current* view again.

'Well, you'll soon see for yourself, won't you?'

What was bugging *him*? Because Merrow could spot a cool tone from fifty paces, even from someone she barely knew. Hadn't she just got his sweet, perfectly formed ass out of the fire yesterday? Where was the charm he had promised?

'Does your father still come to Dublin now that he's retired?'

There was a small, low burst of laughter in response to that. 'Oh, I think you'll find he uses the term "retired" very loosely. But he rarely comes to Dublin.'

'He must trust your judgement to leave you in charge.'

'*That* I had to work for.'

Was that why the Pavenham was so important? Was he proving a point? But before she could ask he was pushing open another door and she found herself walking into a light, airy living space that seemed to stretch endlessly to either side of her. There hadn't been the smallest hint that a place like Alex's apartment even existed behind the Georgian front of the building. But judging by the space, it was more than the one building...

'How many houses do you have here?'

'Three.' He walked ahead of her into the open kitchen before glancing at her from the corner of his eye, one large hand lifting a bottle of wine off the counter. 'Do you want a glass of wine?'

Well, she wasn't driving...

'Please.' She walked to the other side of the counter and set her portfolio down on the dark granite surface, slipping her bag off her shoulder to lay it alongside while her eyes scanned the room. 'This place is amazing.'

'I remodelled about a year ago. When the property next door came on the market I bought it and knocked through. The lower floors of the new building hold a design school now.'

Not living under the old man's shadow so much, then. Alex was already carving out his own niche. And there was something sexy about that too. He was his own man.

'Your dad must be very proud of what you've done.'

Alex shrugged his broad shoulders as he uncorked the

wine, his gaze focussed on the task so she couldn't read his expression. Not that she had proved too good at that so far. He really did play the strong, silent type very well.

'He hasn't seen it.'

In a year? Her eyebrows rose as he poured into a deep-bowled glass, the red wine swirling like liquid silk. He glanced up at her, his hazel gaze flickering briefly back and forth from each of her eyes before he smiled a hint of a smile and passed the glass to her.

'Like I said, he rarely comes to Dublin.'

Her fingertips brushed against his on the glass, and the shock wave reached all the way to her toes, so electrically charged that she almost gasped. And as the charge tingled to her already heated core, her gaze flew upwards and locked with his, his eyes narrowing a barely perceptible amount. Did that mean he'd felt it too? He was just so much more guarded than she remembered him being in Galway!

But two could play at that game. So she smiled and drew the glass back towards her body. 'Thank you.'

'You're welcome.'

While he poured another glass, Merrow walked around the living area, drawn to a wall covered with photographs in varying different frames. There were a lot of rather well-composed shots of landscapes and city scapes and buildings. But scattered amongst them were pictures of Alex. Alex skiing, Alex with his arms held out to his sides about to fall off a bridge with a bungee rope around his ankles, Alex sailing. My, how the other half lived!

And he had varying grins or had been caught 'mid-laughter' in nearly every one, which made her glance across at him as he came out of the kitchen, to compare them to his cool expression in the here and now.

Judging by the vast difference, he didn't like her much, did he? And she was inexplicably a little hurt by that thought. Most people considered her quite nice to be around…and surely liking each other a little would make it easier to work together?

And it didn't cross the business and pleasure boundary. Because, with a great deal of thought, she knew that to hop in the sack with Galway Alex was a hellishly different decision from hopping in the sack with Alexander Fitzgerald. Galway Alex couldn't affect her career for decades to come. The wrong words in the right ears from Alexander Fitzgerald could have her eating pasta and rice for a long, long time…

'Did you get badges for doing all these activities, like in the boy scouts?'

His mouth quirked again as he got closer, his eyes sparkling. 'No. But then I'm no boy scout.'

Walked into that one, didn't she?

He stood beside her, glanced at her from the corner of his eye, and then focussed on the photos. 'As *you* well know.'

She watched as he lifted his glass and took a sip of wine. She watched his throat convulse as he swallowed, watched his chest rise and fall as he took a breath. And for the life of her she couldn't find a reason to look away, especially when he licked the taste of the wine off his lips.

Oh, my, the things he had done to her with that tongue…

Eventually he turned towards her, inches separating them while Merrow looked directly into his eyes.

Alex studied her face, calmly took another sip of wine, then nodded, just the once. 'How's your wine?'

Merrow looked down at the glass, swirled the liquid around the bowl, lifting it to the light as she tilted her head to study the colour. 'Nice deep colour.'

From her peripheral vision she saw his mouth quirk.

Lowering the glass, she held it beneath her nose and breathed in. 'Mmm…a slight hint of blackberry on the nose… maybe oak?'

With an eyebrow quirked in challenge, she fixed her gaze on his over the rim of the glass and took a sip, crinkling her nose and smiling as she swallowed. 'Yummy.'

'Not a wine connoisseur, then.'

'Not so much.' She smiled when he finally cracked a smile, the gold glow in his eyes warming her body from the outside as the rich liquid warmed her from within. 'I know when one tastes good, and this one does, but then I wouldn't expect less from someone like you. I always look at the alcohol content first myself. And I might need a few oysters with this for it to have the full effect…'

Alex didn't miss the Galway innuendo, his head tilting a little to the side. 'You really do like playing with fire, don't you?'

'I have a mischievous streak a mile wide, I'm told.'

'Are you really as confident as you come across?'

'I work very hard at trying to be. But then in order to be confident you have to know your own limitations too. And I'm fully aware of my failings.' She shrugged one shoulder. 'I just choose not to make them public. Works for me.'

'As does using your sexuality to manage a difficult client?'

Her smile faded. 'Yes, I was wondering when we'd get to that. You lasted a whole ten minutes, well done.'

'It's what you did.'

'It's what it took. You said he was being difficult and to be honest it wasn't something I hadn't already heard about him. So I used what I had. It wasn't like I offered my naked body up on a silver platter for his delectation.'

'He's old enough to be your father.'

'My mother was enough of a fan to have had a go at that

idea back in the day.' Merrow moved away from him, wandering aimlessly around the room, cradling the bowl of her glass in her palm. 'But fortunately for me she loved my dad the day she set eyes on him. I doubt Mickey D would've made as good a father. Sex, babies and rock and roll doesn't have quite the same ring to it.'

'And is that how you sell all your ideas for design to a client?'

That's it, Alex, be an ass. She took a deep breath and turned on her heel to frown at him from across the room. 'What is it exactly that you dislike so much about me, Alex? Is it the fact that a woman had a one-night stand with you on equal terms? Or is it the fact that a woman found it easier to sell a vision to a reputedly sex-mad rock star better than you because you don't happen to have breasts?'

His jaw clenched briefly. 'And what makes you so sure I dislike you?'

He got her with that one, for a split second. 'Oh, I dunno, maybe the fact that you're such a joy when I'm around?'

His dark blond brows quirked. 'You have an innate ability to intrigue and irritate me in equal measure, often at the same time, as it happens, but if you recall that didn't seem to hold me back any in Galway. And when it comes to that night, you should maybe consider for a moment that I'm not the kind of guy that does one-night stands on as regular a basis as you'd like to think. So not liking you isn't the issue.'

What?

For the first time in a long time, Merrow was at a loss for words. And the fact that she floundered brought the smile briefly back onto Alex's face. Then it faded.

'I told you that first day I didn't want the fact we slept together to get in the way. But the fact is it's damn well *in* the way. And it'll *stay* in the way if you make the Pavenham

Project a daily foray into the world of seduction. It needs to stop—unless you want to face the consequences.'

Merrow's shoulders dropped, and, even though she could feel a wave of sexual excitement tingling over her nerve endings, she was also swamped by a sense of artistic disappointment. 'You hated my ideas, didn't you?'

Alex stunned her by chuckling, and when she looked at him he shook his head, a softer smile curving his lips. 'No, Merrow, I didn't hate your ideas. In fact if the sketches in that portfolio even half live up to what you sold to Mickey yesterday, then I think we're in business.'

Okay, now she was just plain old confused!

'Then what's the problem here again?'

The smile faded, his chin dropped, the wine swirling in the glass as he carefully worded his reply in a deep rumbling tone. 'The problem is I can't do business the way you did it yesterday. This firm has a reputation to protect and—'

'You thought I was unprofessional?'

'No, I found your method—'

'A little too much like prostitution for your taste?' Oh, he was walking a *very* thin line now.

He immediately locked gazes with her, a frown on his forehead. 'I didn't say that.'

'You think I cheapened myself somehow and that might sully the professional image of the great Fitzgerald & Son by association?'

And why that thought hurt so much she had *no idea!* Who did he think he was?

'I didn't say *that* either.' He waggled a long finger at her in warning. 'Don't put words in my mouth. What I was trying to say, before you started jumping to conclusions, was that this company has always had a certain way of doing things, and your off-the-wall methods would work better for me with a little more warning. I'd prefer not to have to stand there and watch some aged womaniser drooling over your every word. The way he was looking at you, you may as well have been doing the dance of the seven veils for him!'

Merrow pursed her lips together and looked away from him, tapping one foot on the floor while she tried to control her anger.

'What now?'

She shook her head, thrusting the end of her tongue against the inside of one cheek while she tried to decide why it was she was still standing there.

Because she *wanted this job*—dammit! She'd barely stopped sketching and collaging since she'd left the hotel. Because he was right in what he'd said the day he'd come looking for her. There wasn't an interior designer who *wouldn't* be turned on by this project!

'Just say whatever it is you're thinking and we can get the air cleared before we start working together.'

'Maybe I don't want to work with you.' And she didn't give a stuff if that came out petulantly.

'I saw how you were talking about it yesterday—'

'Yes—' she glared at him '—so you've just *said*!'

He took a deep breath. 'You were excited by it. Your whole face lit up. And that's exactly the kind of passion I want from the person working on this.'

'Just so long as I don't sell that passion to the client, right?'

'Just so long as that's the *only* passion you try selling to *any* client of mine.'

Son-of-a—

Hang on a minute. Her jaw dropped in realization. 'You were *jealous*?'

He pursed his mouth into a tight line and glared at her in

warning as he marched towards the kitchen. And for one ridiculous moment Merrow felt like giggling like a schoolgirl. *He was jealous?* Mr Hotness himself, who could probably have any woman he chose on the entire island thanks to his wealth and family, was jealous she'd flirted a teensy ikkle bit with Mickey D to get him on board with her ideas?

If someone had even suggested that to her twenty-four hours ago she'd have answered them with an astounded, *'Shut up!'*

As it was, a tiny part of her felt a real need to do a happy dance in the middle of his living room. Which was just plain silly, because she'd already decided it'd be a bad idea to mix business and pleasure with Alex Fitzgerald, hadn't she? *Bad Merrow.*

She turned on her heel and set her glass on the counter, tilting her chin to look up into his eyes. 'Why would you be jealous, Alex? It's not like we're in any kind of a relationship.'

'No, we're not—' he said the words in a curt, matter-of-fact tone, his expression deadpan '—but I'd like to continue to believe that night in Galway was something you didn't do too often either, if that's all right with you.'

She nodded, her heart thudding faster in her chest. 'Ever, as it happens. You were my first one-night stand. Congratulations.'

The gold in his eyes blazed in response. And she could see the old temptation of a hinted smile twitch the corners of his mouth. So she damped her lips with the end of her tongue and watched as he watched the movement. It really was terribly empowering. And it played to her wicked streak no end…

'But it *was* an incredible night.'

'It was.'

Merrow took a breath, her breasts rising and falling with the action, which grazed her suddenly sensitive nipples against the lace of her bra. 'But we're not in a relationship and to be honest I have a very full and busy life. I don't really have time for something serious. I'm only twenty-seven and I'd like to make a success of my career first. I'm greedy that way.'

'I get that. I'm the same and I'm not that much older than you.' But the hint of a smile was taking hold, and continuing holding his gaze while the gold blazed even hotter in his eyes was getting tough to do. It was like staring directly into the sun.

She tilted her head to one side in thought, studying where his dark shirt touched the side of his broad neck. 'So unless we decided to have some kind of hot, steamy affair for the duration of the project, there wouldn't really be any point in you going all jealous lover on me—' she looked back into his eyes '—would there?'

His eyes narrowed, but the smile remained, even with the hooded gaze. He wasn't actually going to confess to being jealous, Merrow got that. But he hadn't actually denied it either. And judging by the heat crackling the air around them, she wasn't the only one turned on right that second. It was just like last time.

Except this time there weren't any oysters to blame as aphrodisiacs…

She tilted her head the other way, considering just how completely insane she wanted to be. 'Okay, then.'

Alex reached for a piece of carrot, popping it into his mouth and chewing while he watched her with cautious eyes as she walked around the counter. He swallowed, folding his arms across his dark shirt as she got closer. '*Now* what are you doing?'

'Consider it an experiment.' She wrapped her hand around the back of his neck, stood up on tiptoe and pressed her mouth to his.

CHAPTER FOUR

ALEX froze.

When they were handing out sexy in heaven Merrow had been top of the queue, hadn't she? She might have skipped the subtlety and shyness queues, but he wasn't complaining. He'd had enough of the kinds of women who played games.

He let her lead the tempo for a while, just to see how far she would go. But he helped her out some by unfolding his arms so she could press her breasts against the wall of his chest, and he gripped the edge of the counter behind him to steady them. While her soft, hot little mouth moved over his in a teasing whisper of a kiss, her eyes open and focussed on his.

But when she tugged his bottom lip between hers and gently nipped on it with her teeth, he'd had enough. If she was prepared to play with fire...and he'd said there would be consequences...

So he lifted his hands off the counter and snaked his arms around her waist, his fingers splaying as he smoothed down from the small of her back to her backside, where he cupped her and hauled her in tight against the rapidly growing ridge pressing against the zipper of his jeans.

Her luminous eyes widened in surprise, and he smiled against her mouth before angling his head, deepening the kiss, his tongue tracing the gap in her lips so that she opened wider, allowing him access to the recesses of her mouth. When her heavy eyelids dropped, he closed his eyes, his tongue tangling with hers while his fingertips teased the edge of her short skirt higher.

She moaned into his mouth, he felt her nipples pebble against his chest, and the smile inside his chest grew. Oh, yeah, little Miss Merrow O'Connell might run rings round him during the working day, but this was *his* territory. And so long as she reacted this fast when he touched her, he had the advantage, didn't he?

His fingertips touched soft, rounded skin. And he groaned low in his chest. Didn't the woman ever wear underwear that wasn't there specifically to torture him? He leaned forwards a little, arching her backwards as his forefinger traced under the narrow line of her lace G-string, while he shifted his hips, pushing a knee between hers to nudge her legs a little wider for easier access. But as his searching fingertip got closer to her heated centre, she wrenched her mouth from his and stepped back out of his hold, her eyelids heavy, her lips swollen, her cheeks flushed.

And Alex smiled a slow, lazy, triumphant smile at her. 'Something wrong?'

Merrow's eyes narrowed the tiniest amount, before she ran her tongue over her reddened lips and lifted her chin. 'I think we've just established there's absolutely nothing *wrong*. I swear, you should wear a danger sign.'

'You were the one who suggested an affair.' He was still smiling as he reached for his wineglass.

But as he took a sip her chin rose higher, and he saw the challenge spark in her eyes before she spoke. 'An affair is all it would be, Alex, 'cos your world and mine?' She waved a hand between them. 'A never-the-twain-shall-meet kinda thing. Seriously. I jest you not.'

His glass froze halfway up to his mouth. What exactly did *that* mean?

But before he could ask, she smiled that mischievous imp of a smile again, the Galway version, that spoke of making mischief on a very adult level. 'Just so long as you understand that…'

She turned and glanced down the hallway that ran off the kitchen, her hands reaching to her side for the zipper of her dress. 'Which way?'

Alex's heart thumped up against his ribs, hard, his mouth suddenly dry. 'To where?'

He heard the soft rasp of the zip as she tugged it down, his feet carrying him forwards to follow her as she shrugged out of one shoulder, glancing back over her shoulder to inform him, 'The bedroom, of course. I get the feeling that granite surface might be a bit chilly under me if you set me on the counter.'

Well, if he hadn't already been turned on—

'Merrow—'

She turned on her heel and leaned a hand against the wall as she toed one shoe off, her arched brows rising in question. 'Alex?'

Alex felt his palms itch. If she was kidding she had about ten seconds to tell him she was kidding. After that he wouldn't be held accountable for his own actions. 'Just like that? Again?'

She shrugged the naked shoulder as she toed the other shoe off. 'Well, it's not like this is going anywhere, is it? You were the one who said it was in the way. So let's get it out of the way.'

Alex set his glass on the end of the counter, walking towards her as he shoved his hands into his pockets. 'You don't have to do this to get the job. You'll get that on talent.'

She scowled at that, standing tall on her bare feet while she folded her arms across her breasts and tilted her head, which made him smile, because attempting to look angry with him would have worked much better if she hadn't been half undressed already.

'I'm gonna let that one slide, 'cos you really don't know me. This is nothing to do with work. And I *am* talented enough for the job. You'll see that when you bother looking at the portfolio. This is about *this*. I want you. Judging by the present you have for me in your jeans, you want me too. It's an itch. That's all. But it's in the way.'

'An *itch*?'

Her eyes darkened as he kept walking towards her, then she unfolded her arms and backed away, her hand lifting to draw the other side of her dress off her shoulder. 'Sex is sex, Alex.'

He didn't know why he wanted to know, and, to be honest, was *an idiot* to want to know when she was handing him what he wanted on a plate, without any commitment, but... 'Someone did a real number on you, didn't they?'

The flush rose on her cheeks, even as she laughed. 'There doesn't have to be anything behind it. Why can't a woman play a man's game? So long as you play safe there's no reason why you shouldn't reach out for something you want. I'm not in a relationship, not that that stops a man...'

And in that statement he knew what he needed to know. 'Is that what he did? Did he cheat on you?'

She faltered briefly, then continued walking backwards, distracting him by letting the dress slide down over her breasts, revealing enough white lace and pink bows to make Alex groan aloud.

'This has nothing to do with anyone else, Alex. This has to do with you and me, just like it did last time.' She reached behind her back, the movement pushing her breasts up and forwards as she unhooked her bra and shrugged the straps off her shoulder, letting them slide slowly down her arms before it hit the floor.

'Seeing you reminded me how good we were together. Don't you remember that? Don't you remember how it felt?'

Alex swallowed hard, the husky words doing as much damage to his self-control as the sight of her hands lifting to her throat, where she splayed her fingers over her skin before running her palms down over her breasts, over the curve of her flat stomach, pushing the dress down over her hips.

'I remember everything.'

'Well, if you remember...' she shimmied her hips, and the pale green and blue plaid pooled at her feet '...how can you not want to get lost like that again?'

Was that what she wanted to do—to get lost for a while? Lost from what—and why with him? What shift in luck had brought this kind of offering to his apartment after so many months of working every hour that God sent? Because she'd been right that first day when she'd offered him tea; he *was* tense. He'd been tense for months, had felt as if he had the weight of the world on his shoulders and, quite frankly, had days when he could have spent hours in front of the punch bag at his local gym. This seemed like a much better option to him...

If a part of him didn't feel as if he'd be using her.

She stepped towards him in all her practically naked glory, her hips moving from side to side in a sensual sway that Alex very much doubted she knew she was doing. So he stayed still and waited for her to get to him, which just happened to be beside his bedroom door, but he doubted she knew that either.

When she got to him, she studied the column of his neck again, her fingers lifting to smooth a line from behind his ear into the collar of his shirt. 'You're so tense, Alex. You weren't this tense in Galway. I did offer you chamomile tea, but you didn't want any...'

He pursed his lips to hold back a smile when she tilted her

head to look up at him again, her eyes sparkling with the oh-so-familiar mischief. She was a temptress, this one.

'He was a bloody idiot.'

Her eyes widened in question as he dragged his hands out of his pockets and reached for her hands, lifting them above her head as he pushed her back against the wall. 'Who was?'

Alex ducked his head, and ran his mouth along the beating pulse in her neck, drawing a gasp from her lips as he leaned in and the material of his shirt grazed her nipples. 'Whoever it was felt he had to play away when he had this at home.'

And whoever he'd been, Alex was determined to erase every memory of him from her. If she was going to offer him a no-strings affair then he was going to give her some *very* special memories to replace any bad ones.

She arched her back off the wall when he ran his tongue along her shoulder blade, sighed softly when he nipped her skin. And when her head dropped forward and she rested her forehead against his shoulder, he took a deep breath, and smelled the lavender on her hair.

Who was he kidding? He could *try* and be honourable, but he wanted her so bad that he ached, his hips jerking when she rubbed her abdomen across the front of his jeans. 'Last chance to change your mind, O'Connell.'

Merrow turned her head to whisper into his ear. 'I want you. *Inside me.*'

He looped her hands around his neck, freeing his hands to lift her off her feet, her long legs wrapping around his waist as he pressed her into the wall and tilted his head back to reach up and kiss her, their mouths fusing together. He braced his feet wider apart, using the wall and his body to support her as he pulled the soft bands off the ends of her braids, running his fingers through them until her hair was loose around her face, then he threaded them in deep, cradling her head, massaging her scalp as he tangled his tongue with hers again, as he drew her bottom lip into his mouth and nipped playfully the same way she had in the kitchen.

She mumbled against his mouth, 'You have too many clothes on for this.'

Alex chuckled. 'So do you.'

Not that the scrap of white lace she still had on constituted clothing. But it was still in the way. And with her ankles hooked firmly behind him, there was no way of removing it. But there was time yet...

He let his fingers slide out of her hair, let them whisper over her jaw, down her neck, over her shoulders, then in a waving dance over her breasts until he cupped them both, kneading as he ran his thumbs over her nipples. She writhed back, broke the kiss, her even white teeth biting down on her lip.

And he smiled at her again. 'Good?'

'Mmm...'

He pushed his hips up so that the ridge of his zipper brushed against the tiny scrap of lace covering her core. And smiled again when she moaned.

'More?'

'Uh-huh.'

He chuckled as he reached for the door handle beside them. 'You know, if this is what it takes to get you to stop talking I might have to do this a lot more.'

She wrapped her legs and her arms tighter around him as he supported her backside and carried her into the room, her head tilting to rain kisses along the side of his face until she got back to his mouth. 'Are you saying I talk too much?'

'I'm saying sometimes you don't need words.'

'Show me,' she mumbled against his mouth.

Alex had had every intention of being suave, lowering her gently to the bed, but it didn't quite work out that way. With her mouth tangled with his and him trying to dump his shoes off by the bed, gravity got in the way, so he stumbled and just about managed to shift his weight before he crushed her on the bed.

Merrow giggled as she swung one leg over his hips. 'Slick.'

'I know.' He chuckled back, one hand tangling in her hair again, drawing her in for a kiss that ended in her gasp as his other hand sneaked down between them and fingered the lace to one side so he could slide into her moist heat. 'Slick would definitely be the word.'

'You have that effect on me.'

The thought of Merrow in a permanent state of readiness for him did things to Alex's libido he couldn't remember being done in a long while.

She leaned back on her knees, using one hand to support herself so he could keep touching her while she unhooked the buttons of his shirt with her other hand. When they were all undone and he could see the flush growing on her cheeks from his long-fingered teasing, she frowned a little, bit down on her lip, and he couldn't resist thumbing some of her moisture over her most sensitive place.

'Oh-h-h!' She bucked against his hand.

Hell. Some guy seriously thought he could get more fun elsewhere? Really? What kind of a moron was he?

'Easy.'

'I'm not the one making it happen.'

She leaned forwards again, her hands roving over the hard wall of his chest and making him suck in his breath as she moved lower, her knuckles sliding against his abdomen as she popped the button of his jeans and reached for the zipper. He drew her head down again, kissed her slow and deep and long, used his tongue to mimic what he planned on doing to her.

'Protection?'

'Side table drawer.' He smiled against her mouth when she reached an arm out and couldn't quite touch it. 'We'll have to move.'

'I can get it. Hold on to me.'

And he'd thought he was in charge this time? Obediently he removed his fingers, setting both hands around her narrow waist and tilting his head up off the covers to watch as she leaned back and twisted, his eyes straying briefly to the ceiling as he silently thanked whoever was responsible for flexible women. But it was still too far, so with a murmur of discontent she lifted her leg off him and sidled to the edge of the bed, which worked out okay as far as Alex was concerned, 'cos it gave him time to dump the rest of his clothes while watching from the corner of his eye as she slid the white lace off and threw it towards the door with her foot before he held a hand out.

'I'll do it. I'll be quicker.'

'Practise makes perfect, huh?' She grinned at him, her eyes dancing. 'Not this time, stud.'

Alex almost choked when she reached for him, her hand stroking him as she swung her leg back over him, leaving enough space for her to roll the condom into place. Her hair fell forwards, shrouding her face, so he lifted his hands and smoothed it back, watching her bite her lip in concentration while he felt himself straining up into her hand.

He was *so* not in charge of this. But there was something incredibly sexy about a confident woman who took hold of the situation at hand—literally.

When she was done, she lifted her chin, her palms flattening on his chest, moving up behind his neck, her eyes darkening as she locked gazes with him, shifting her hips forwards, rocking, so that her slick heat teased him to breaking-point, before she sank down onto him, inch by torturous inch.

Her lips parted, her breathing sped up. And Alex watched the play of emotions in the depths of her eyes as he filled her, her moist heat surrounding him.

Damn, but she was amazing.

She chuckled at his expression, the sound vibrating down to where their bodies were connected, so that every sensitive inch of Alex ached so bad it was almost painful. 'You're officially killing me.'

Merrow leaned in and kissed him, open-eyed, her pelvis beginning to rock as she whispered against his lips, *'Le petit mort.* That's what they used to call it, you know.'

'I'm starting to get why.' Having already witnessed some of her flexibility, Alex freed her face and pushed against his elbows until he was upright, and Merrow reached her hands back to rest them on his knees, arching her spine as she rocked her pelvis. So Alex adjusted his weight onto one palm, used the other to palm her breast, to run his fingertips over each of her ribs, until he could get a finger back to her sensitive nub.

She bucked a little—sank back down on him—rocked harder. And even as he felt the pressure building in his abdomen he watched her face, the flush that had travelled down from her cheeks and onto her neck, how her bottom lip was paler as she bit it harder, while she made small, moaning sighs that drove him to the brink.

Had he thought amazing? As he fought to stop himself from hitting the edge before her he knew it wasn't a big enough word. Not by a long shot.

She locked gazes with him, and something inside his chest ached as she smiled. The same way it had ached the first time they had been joined together this way. Like some kind of weird connection to her that he'd never felt before. It was why he remembered that one night so clearly, had never forgotten any of it.

She lifted a hand from one knee, wrapped it tight around the column of his neck and rocked harder. She was close, he could feel her body tightening around him, so he swirled his finger in the moisture he could reach, flicking his fingertip back and forth, once, twice, over the bundle of sensitized nerve endings.

'*Al-ex!*' She closed her eyes and breathed out his name, her body convulsing around his hard length, drawing him in further, squeezing, until he couldn't stop the rush for release, his own groan of satisfaction low and guttural.

Oh, yeah, she was gonna be the death of him, all right.

She rested her head on his shoulder for a long while, their ragged breathing filling the silence as Alex lay back flat on the bed, drawing her with him before he settled his arms around her, his hands smoothing the soft skin on her back as she sighed against his neck.

'We're good at this.'

'That we are.' He kept smoothing his fingers over her skin, the scent of lavender right by his nose. And suddenly he wasn't at all tense any more.

Actually he felt pretty damn fine.

She lifted her head off his shoulder and kissed him, soft and slow, before stunning him by brightly announcing, 'I gotta go. I'm going to be late.'

Whoa, wait a minute!

He tightened his arms around her when she tried to get up. 'Where are you going?'

'I'm meeting my friends in Temple Bar.'

He frowned. 'Oh, really?'

'Yep.' She smiled as if it weren't a problem. 'It's Lisa's birthday, so we're going for drinks.'

'Now?' She was running out on him? 'So now the itch is scratched you're off to party?'

Pathetically it made him feel used.

'I had it planned before I knew this would happen. Not that I *knew* this would happen. In fact…' she settled more comfortably on his chest and searched a point above his head with her green eyes before locking gazes again '…I was fairly determined this *wasn't* going to happen. But there ya go—best laid plans and all that…'

Alex relaxed his arms a little. 'So what made you change your mind?'

She butted the end of her nose off his and grinned. 'Apparently I've always had a problem keeping my hands off you.'

He had absolutely no complaints about that, so he merely cleared his throat. 'We-ell, I guess I can't really blame you for *that*—ow!'

She set the elbow she'd nudged him with on the duvet and propped her head on her hand as he chuckled. 'You see, now *this* is the guy I remember from Galway. Dublin Alex is uptight, he's tense. I wasn't sure I liked him so much for a little while.'

He realised he was smoothing his hands over her skin again. She wasn't the only one having difficulty with keeping hands off, was she? 'Not so tense any more, as it happens.'

Merrow went silent for a moment, and when he looked into her eyes the green had softened from the usual sparkling shade of emerald green to a warm shade of mossy-green. He smoothed his hands again and smiled a slow smile, his voice husky.

'What?'

'This project really means a lot to you, doesn't it?'

'Yes, it does.' He exhaled the truth.

'Why?'

She took the weight off her knees and laid out flat, so that she was stretched along the length of his body from the breasts squished against his chest, all the way down to the feet she was playing footsie with. And even though Alex could feel himself slowly sliding from the cocoon of her core, he already felt the stirring response that having her naked skin pressed to his naked skin was invoking.

She even dragged her fingernails along the skin of his arm and made his pulse jump. Another couple of minutes and she wasn't going anywhere…

'It just does.' He took a hand off her back and tucked her hair behind her ear.

But she simply tilted her head and it swung free again. 'Why?'

He frowned for a moment. 'If I make conversation with you are you gonna skip going to Temple Bar?'

'No.'

He'd have frowned again, if there hadn't been a note of regret in her voice. 'I can't, Alex, really I can't. It's her thirtieth, it's a big deal. And she's my best friend; we've been there for each other through a lot of stuff.'

Stuff like the ass that cheated on her? Had she had her heart broken? Was that why she now tried to play at sex the 'man's way': free and easy and no involvement?

'But we have months working together on the Pavenham, don't we?'

'Yes, we do.' He tucked her hair back in place when she tilted her head back the other way.

'Well, then.' She leaned in and kissed him again, briefer this time. 'If you want to play again, we have plenty of time.

And maybe I'll get a chance to wheedle out some of your deep, dark secrets along the way.'

He smiled. Unlikely. But it might be fun letting her try.

Another kiss, and this time when she pushed upright he let her go, leaning up on his elbows to study her naked body from head to toe. 'There's a shower next door if you want it.'

Turning her perfect naked butt to him, she winked over her shoulder. 'I think I'll keep your scent on me so I don't forget this too fast. And if I'm much later there'll be too many questions. Somehow I don't think the idea of four women marking you out of ten would sit well with you.'

'It wouldn't.'

'Thought so.' She disappeared out of the door, so Alex sat up and located his jeans, hauling them on and zipping them, but not bothering with the button as he followed her into the hall in time to watch her shimmy back into her dress, pushing her shoes on at the same time. He smiled at the sight of her with her flushed cheeks, swollen lips and mussed-up hair.

Her friends would have to have guide dogs not to know what she'd been at. He leaned over and lifted the soft rings that had held her braids in place, sauntering up to offer them dangling off the end of his fingers.

'You need to do something with your hair.'

She smiled as she took the bands off his fingers, standing on her toes to kiss him again. 'I know. Someone messed it up on me.'

He hauled her closer and kissed her properly, just so she didn't forget what they'd just shared, smiling against her mouth when she moaned in frustration. 'Just so you know, if you'd stayed, we weren't done.'

With her eyes still closed, she rocked back on her heels,

running the tip of her tongue over her lips as if she was savouring the taste of him. 'Mmm. I know.'

'Well, maybe you should come back for brunch tomorrow and I'll tell you what I thought of your sketches and we'll… see…what…happens…'

He left the suggestion hanging in the air, a chuckle bubbling up from deep in his chest when she opened her eyes, smiled her mischievous imp smile and swung her shoulders back and forth. 'I *love* brunch.'

Alex shook his head and waved the back of his hand in a flapping motion down the hall. 'Go on, then. Just leave me. Go play with your friends. I'll be fine, don't you worry.'

Merrow giggled, backing away from him until she got to the kitchen and reached for her bag, pushing out her lower lip before she crooned, 'Poor baby.'

Alex opened the door and leaned on it, jerking his head. 'Go.'

When she made an attempt to scoot through the door, he cleared his throat, loudly. So she stepped back a step, ran her palms up over his naked chest, wrapped her arms round his neck, and kissed him on the damn cheek.

He shook his head as she jogged down the stairs. 'Hey, O'Connell?'

'Yes?' She tilted her head back, her fingers braiding her hair as she smiled up at him.

'So what *was* my score out of ten?'

'Ah-h-h…' Her fingers continued braiding at breakneck speed. 'You see, I prefer to take an average score overall. So I might need to get back to you on that.'

Alex felt his mouth twitch. 'Stay outta trouble.'

'Go look at my sketches.'

'I intend to.'

'I'll see you tomorrow.'

CHAPTER FIVE

TOMORROW ran into another tomorrow and another tomorrow. And pretty soon Merrow realised the days seemed to be flowing into each other at an almost frightening speed. It wasn't anything overly out of the norm when it came to her life, but the way that spending time with Alex was fitting in so neatly with the usual chaos was, *unexpected*. Almost a little *too right*.

And he really wasn't so tense any more. Playing hard *as well* as working hard seemed to be doing him good.

But then Merrow liked to think she was helping with that. Though in fairness there was still work to do.

'You do know you change when you put on a suit?'

Her eyes scanned the dark navy of what was no doubt a designer label suit, which, granted, he looked good enough to eat in, but it also gave him an air of 'all-businesslike' that she desperately wanted to *ruffle*. Even if he *had* softened his appearance some by loosening his tie, undoing the top button of his pale blue shirt and walking by her side with his hands in his pockets.

The corners of Alex's mouth quirked, the gold flecks shining bright in the hazel when he looked at her from the corner of his eye. 'Really.'

He didn't make it a question, but then Merrow had noticed how he'd taken to letting her ramble on for a while or get to her point before he either contradicted her or distracted her off the topic. It was a clever ploy. But then Alex Fitzgerald was nobody's fool. She liked that about him.

'Yup.' She nudged his upper arm with her shoulder and grinned at him as she bit on the corner of her lip. 'You go all stuffy, serious Dublin Alex on me.'

He leaned his head a little to the side so that only she could hear his low-spoken words. 'Ah-h-h, but then I have you to loosen me up later, don't I?'

'Yes.' Her gaze fixed on the curve of his mouth, the mouth that was capable of *so* much. 'That you most definitely do.'

He read the look in her eyes and surprised her by twisting round on his heels to duck down and place a swift kiss on her lips, mumbling the promise of, 'Later'—before he lifted a hand out of one pocket to haul open the door to the restaurant and set that one large hand on the small of her back to guide her inside. As free as they were with touching each other, at length, in private, public shows of affection weren't something either of them had done much of.

Merrow had been quite pleased about that. Or she'd told herself she was. Because this was still an affair, they weren't 'dating' and they most definitely weren't a 'couple'; she'd made that clear. And Alex didn't seem to have a problem with it either, which was great.

He certainly didn't have any problem with the 'affair' part of an affair. In fact brunch was now officially her favourite time of the day—'brunch' being a secret codeword for getting together to 'mess around,' that was.

Of course there was after official working hours too, when they would meet up to eat something at his place and chat about the progress at the Pavenham before messing around some more...

In fact, this was the first time he'd insisted they eat somewhere with people. Which Merrow told herself wasn't a date. It was just handy, because the restaurant was halfway between the Pavenham and his place and he'd insisted he was in the mood for Italian.

See? All fine. Because, really, there was no point in getting their two worlds all tangled up in something that wouldn't last.

The restaurant owner greeted Alex by name and immediately guided them past the queue of people waiting for tables. One of the perks of being a Fitzgerald, Merrow supposed. But halfway through the crowded room there was a loud, 'Oh, my God,' swiftly followed by a, *'Merrow! Over here!'*

Her heart sank. Oh, no. Not *the gang!*

She glanced briefly at the bemused expression on Alex's face before she turned round to look at the three familiar faces wearing matching ecstatic grins. And she answered them with a tight lipped, tilted head, wide-eyed glare of recrimination before Alex stepped in beside her, his hand on the small of her back again,

'Hello, ladies.'

'Well, hello!' Lisa waved a hand from across the table. 'How nice to see you again.'

'Again?' Alex quirked his brows in question.

'Oh, you probably don't remember. We were all at the Oyster Festival with Merrow that night in Galway.'

Merrow could quite happily have had a hole appear in the floor in front of her. A large one. And she'd have waved byebye on her way in.

'What are you guys doing here?' Normally this kind of a gathering was news she was informed about. If they were all meeting behind her back to discuss how the tag-teaming was going she was going to make them all suffer.

'Gracie won big on a Lotto scratch card at lunch time so we're all here spending it. You'd know that if you bothered answering your phone. But we just assumed you were *busy*.'

Another glare from Merrow earned a tacked on, 'With the hotel thing and all that.'

Nice save.

'I take it these are the other three musketeers?' The sound of Alex's deep voice close to her left ear dragged her gaze back to his face, where she found a silent amusement sparkling in his eyes.

She nodded dumbly in response.

'You're welcome to join us,' Gracie helpfully piped up. 'It's on me. And you can ask us lots of questions about Merrow if you buy the wine.'

Merrow glared again, her Christmas-card list rapidly shortening. 'No, thanks, Gracie, we're just—'

'Lots of questions, you say?' His hand snaked round from the small of her back to the side of her waist, where he squeezed hard. 'Well, that seems like too good an opportunity to miss. But dinner's on me, Gracie, and the wine. You should treat yourself to something with the winnings, shouldn't she, O'Connell?'

Like a nice outfit for her coffin, maybe?

'Alex—'

But Alex had already raised a hand to the restaurant owner and chairs magically appeared as her friends all shuffled round the heavy wooden table to make room.

It was a nightmare. So much for their two worlds never meeting…

He made sure she was seated while her three soon-to-beex-friends all sighed their approval, and then he removed his jacket, tugging his tie loose and shoving it into an inside pocket before he draped the jacket over his chair and sat down, unbuttoning another button as he smiled his most charming smile at his audience.

'Red or white?'

'So are we talking about what's wrong or are we pretending nothing's wrong 'til we get back to my place and I *wheedle* it out of you another way?'

Merrow lifted her chin and continued walking. 'Nothing's wrong.'

'That's okay.' She could hear the amusement in his voice. 'I'm fine with the wheedling option.'

'There's nothing to wheedle.'

'Oh, I think there is.'

'Well, you're wrong.'

Alex pushed his hands back into his pockets and continued walking beside her while Merrow stared down Grafton Street. There was no point in trying to explain how she felt.

Because, to be completely truthful, she hadn't quite sorted through *how* she felt yet. She just knew she was, well, *miffed*, quite frankly.

'I didn't spill any food.'

She ignored him as he withdrew a hand and began holding fingers up as he counted off what he obviously considered to be plus points.

'I used all the right cutlery.'

'There were only two courses,' she mumbled back, 'so it's not like you had that much cutlery to begin with.'

'Still counts, though.' He unfurled another finger. 'I didn't ask for a quarter of the information they supplied me with. *And—*'

He leaned a little closer to add, 'I even deflected a couple of titbits that sounded like they were going to be *really* juicy to help you with your embarrassment…'

He didn't unfurl another finger for that one, Merrow noted. And, in fairness, another bottle of wine and her friends would have divulged enough information to make her contemplate moving to another country.

Another finger unfurled. 'I didn't push for the reasons why I'm apparently much better than "that Dylan one"—who, incidentally, I'm assuming was the prat that cheated on you.'

Probably because she'd barely managed to stifle a moan of mortified agony at that point…

And another finger. 'Even *you* have to admit that I was at my most charming. I didn't even try to feel you up under the table, though the fact you're wearing trousers instead of one of those short skirts I like so much was a help with that—'

'Yes, but you didn't have any problem with smiling at me the whole damn time, or brushing my hair back or holding my hand on the table.' She stopped in the middle of the street and turned to frown up at him. 'Since when have you been so into PDAs?'

His other hand appeared out of his pocket as he stopped and turned to face her, both hands twisting in the air to form an invisible shape as his brows lifted in question. 'Those little hand-held computer things?'

'*No.*' She pursed her lips and shook her head in frustration. '*Public Displays of Affection.* Since when do we do that?'

The hands were tucked in against his broad chest as he folded his arms. 'There's a rule about that I didn't know, is there?'

'Well…' She frowned at a point at the base of his throat. 'Yes…there *is*…'

'Because it breaks the "affair" boundaries, does it?'

'Yes!' She'd have stamped her foot in frustration if she hadn't thought it would've made her look like a five-year-old.

Alex unfolded his arms and stepped a step closer, his voice dropping as he lowered his head. 'You see, I haven't actually been given a list of those rules. So since you're so much more au fait with the whole "affair" thing, then maybe you should fill me in. I've always been the type of guy to wine and dine or actually *date* a woman before this…'

Merrow struggled to find words, which irritated her all the more. How dared he stand there having charmed all her friends to the point of adoration over one meal and then look so gorgeous while pointing out that he was practically God's gift to womankind—and *then* claim to be a *nice guy* too? How was that fair?

When she didn't answer as fast as normal, his brows rose again. 'You have me pegged as some kind of playboy, don't you? Running about all over the country looking for mistresses?'

She sucked her cheeks in.

And Alex smiled his hint of a smile in response. So she frowned and exhaled.

'I hate it when you smile at me like that.'

'No, you don't.'

'I do right this minute.'

He stepped another step closer, tilting his face so close to hers that their foreheads almost touched, his gaze steady and fixed on her eyes. 'You know what I think, O'Connell?'

She searched his glowing eyes, heat radiating all over her body from just that look alone while her pulse bounced erratically. She wasn't actually sure she *did* want to know what he thought, but she sighed and asked anyway.

'What do you think, Alex?'

He angled his head to one side, as if he was about to kiss

her with one of those incendiary kisses of his, right there, in the middle of a busy Grafton Street, in what would end up as a *very* public display…

But instead he kept looking into her eyes as he informed her in a husky whisper, 'I think you need someone to remind you that not every guy on the planet is as big a loser as your last boyfriend was…'

Last boyfriend? Meaning he saw himself as her *current* boyfriend? Hang on a minute—

But before she could call him on it, he leaned back a little, taking a deep breath as he considered a point about an inch above her head, and then he smiled. A wide smile, a devastatingly sexy smile—a smile that addled her brain and distracted her completely from rational thought. Seriously—one man should *not* be allowed to be *that* sexy!

'Meanwhile, having had our first debate in a while, I think we should head back to my place to make up, don't you?'

When she opened her mouth to answer, he stepped back, bent over at the waist, and, to the sound of her surprised squeak, tossed her up over his shoulder.

'Alex! Put me down!'

'Nope.' He hoisted her up a little more as he stood tall, so that her stomach rested on his shoulder, both his arms wrapped around the backs of her knees to hold her in place, and her head dangled upside down facing his back.

Then he started walking down the street.

Merrow heard laughter as they passed people. Scowling, she tried to struggle free, kicking out her feet, 'Put me down!'

'Stop jiggling, woman. You'll make yourself sick after all that food.'

It would serve him right if she threw up all over the back of his designer suit! She attempted to look from side to side, the end of her upside-down pony-tail flicking up into her eyes. 'Alex—'

'Complain all you want, O'Connell.'

'You can't carry me all the way back to your place—you'll have a heart attack.'

'I'll have you know I'm in great physical health, thank you.' She felt his head nod against her hip. 'Good evening, nice night, isn't it?'

And now he was talking to passers-by about the *weather*? She really should've wanted to kill him. But instead she felt a bubble of half-hysterical laughter building in her chest. It was the most ridiculous situation she'd ever found herself in—and that was saying something!

The laughter escaped. 'You are *not* a nice person!'

'I happen to think I'm adorable.'

She laughed again. 'Please put me down, you moron.'

'I'll put you down *on my bed.*'

She moved her head from side to side to see if anyone had heard him, knowing she couldn't blame the heat rising on her cheeks *entirely* on all the blood rushing to her head. But they were already turning off the end of Grafton Street and Alex was marching them past Trinity. He really did have abnormal stamina, didn't he?

You'd have thought she'd have known that already from all the 'messing around' they'd been doing.

Admitting defeat, she attempted to make herself more comfortable for the journey, propping her elbow on his back so she could rest her chin on her hand. She flicked her pony-tail out of the way and when a passing car beeped its horn, she waved at the driver with her free hand, not bothering to look to see if they waved back.

'Hey, Gabe, how you doing?' Alex stopped walking and

Merrow attempted to see who he was talking to. Whoever it was was obviously someone he knew well, judging by the friendly tone of his voice.

A similarly deep voice answered with an amused edge, 'Grand. I've just dropped some estimates through your door for the Gallery job.'

'That was quick.'

'I was out that way this afternoon on another job, so I took a look at the place.' There was a pause. 'So who's your friend?'

Merrow raised her voice. 'Yes, please feel free to introduce me. Or just pretend I'm not here, whatever suits best. Don't mind me.'

'Sorry.' Alex swung round a little. 'Gabriel Burke, Merrow O'Connell. Merrow is the interior designer for the Pavenham. Gabe is the contractor for the project, and an old friend from way back.'

'You have my sympathy.' She reached her hand out and had it shaken by what felt like a ridiculously large hand. She even had to crane her head round to a painful angle to look all the way up at him, 'Wow, you're *tall*, aren't you?'

'Next to this squirt, I am.' Amazingly blue eyes sparkled at her when he leaned down. 'He giving you trouble?'

The six foot one 'squirt'? She sighed dramatically. 'You have *no* idea.'

'You need me to sort him out for you?'

'Would you?'

Alex hoisted her up again. 'When you two have finished flirting with each other…'

Gabe stood tall, his voice laced with a more distinct humour. 'I have to say I'm impressed, squirt. You couldn't have carried her like that when we were kids.'

'She'd have been too big when I was a kid.'

'*Hey!* I'll have you know I'm the ideal weight for my height. I have a colour chart and everything.'

There was the sound of joint male laughter and Merrow felt her stomach jiggled as Alex's shoulders shook. She even giggled herself. There wasn't much else she could do. But they really had gone past the not-tangling-with-each-other's-lives thing if they'd both met each other's friends in the space of a couple of hours. Even if Alex had managed his introductions while the right way up!

Gabe leaned down again. 'Nice meeting you, Merrow. I have a feeling I'll be seeing you again.'

Alex swung her away before she could answer. 'Probably at the party at the tail end of next month—if we don't see you at the hotel.'

'Nah, they don't need me down there. I've moved on to the housing development outside town. So I'll see you both at the party, then.'

'Ash will be back by then. She flies in the day before.'

'Yeah, I know. Bye, Merrow.'

'Bye, Gabe.' She switched elbows and watched him walking down the street as Alex headed for Merrion Square again. 'Do you both come from the land of giant beautiful people?'

He smacked her behind lightly and she flinched. 'What was *that* for?'

'For checking him out enough to think he was beautiful.'

She smiled. 'Is Ash his girlfriend?'

Another smack. 'No, she's my *sister.*'

'You have a sister?'

'That I do. She's been away for a while. You'll meet her at the party.'

Merrow didn't remember being invited to a party. 'What party would that be, then? One of the long list of parties you haven't bothered telling me about? I might not want to go to a party. I might hate parties.'

His shoulder shook again. 'Not according to your friends, you don't. Though if you could avoid going in fancy dress or dancing on any tables at this one that would be helpful. It's my parents' wedding anniversary.'

What? *Oh, no!* She wasn't going to meet his *parents*!

'Alex, put me down!'

'We already discussed that one.'

She struggled again, harder this time. 'I'm not going to any party with you. Especially not one your parents will be at!'

'Breaks another rule, does it?'

'Yes! It does!'

'My father will be fascinated by your plans for the interior—just don't try selling them to him the same way you did with Mickey D. Who will also be there, by the way. Consider it a work-related party.'

And now she felt like a complete idiot for thinking he wanted her to meet his parents. Who did that after less than a fortnight, anyway?

'I'm not going as your *date*.'

'Another rule.' He sighed heavily, the action raising her up and down again. 'You need to be careful or I'll think you're embarrassed being seen with me.'

'Now you're just being ridiculous.' Yes, because being seen in public with the sexiest guy she'd ever met would wreak complete havoc on her reputation, especially when he was a flipping Fitzgerald to boot.

'Well, tell me what the problem is, then.'

'How about we start with the fact that people would perceive us as being a couple when we're *not* a couple?'

'Define a couple for me.'

While he kept on walking, Merrow considered her answer carefully, knowing it was important she worded it right. Because it wasn't that she didn't like Alex, not when everything she'd learnt about him so far had her liking him better with each passing day, but, really—there was no point in thinking about anything beyond hotter-than-Hades, toe-curlingly great sex with him. There really wasn't.

He hoisted her up again. 'Take your time. No rush.'

She squirmed her elbow into his back a little harder and felt him shift his shoulders in response, the tell-tale move bringing a satisfied smirk to her face. 'You really are *not* a nice person.'

'You said.'

Merrow sighed heavily, noticing out of her peripheral vision that they were making remarkably good time getting to his apartment, all things considered…

'A couple is two people, right? In this case a man and a woman…'

He'd apparently given up waiting for her definition. But she didn't grace him with an answer.

'A couple are two people who sleep together. Or rather *don't* sleep together…'

She thought back to the time he'd used the phrase and she'd told him she didn't remember sleeping much. She should've just kept her stupid mouth shut instead of baiting him. Then she wouldn't be in this rapidly growing complicated situation, would she?

She was her own worst enemy sometimes.

'A couple are two people who sleep together but might still be getting to know each other. So, in that case, even though it's early days, they enjoy being round each other enough to want to spend time together.'

Goddamn it!

'But then that might be considered a couple who are *dating*. And we're not doing that, now, are we?'

Finally he was getting it! She sighed. 'Exactly.'

'Because we're just having an *affair*.'

'Yes!'

There was a brief pause. 'Because if you just have an affair then you don't have to take a chance on being hurt by someone you trust again, do you, O'Connell?'

'I *really* want you to put me down now, Alex.'

'We're nearly there.'

They were never, *ever* going to get close to 'there'; that was just the problem. He was way off the mark and yet so close to it at the same time that she felt her heart thudding harder in what could only be fear. He was *dangerous*.

Getting any deeper involved with this man could end up hurting her more than she'd ever been hurt before. But she couldn't tell him that, could she? Not without a long explanation she didn't want to give him.

She knew herself too well to take a chance on him. 'Perfect' couldn't live in the same box as 'chaos'.

'Alex I'm not kidding any more. I want you to put me down and I want to go home.'

He stopped walking, pausing for a long moment while Merrow's heart continued to beat louder and louder. 'Is that what you really want—to run away? Where's the gutsy O'Connell I know so well?'

'After ten days? You don't *know* anyone after ten days!'

'Nor will I if you won't let me *get* to know you.'

'Did you ever hear the one about the pot and the kettle?'

He paused again, his hands moving almost absent-mindedly up and down against the backs of her thighs as he thought about his answer. 'I don't like hiding.'

'And you think that's what we're doing?' She closed her eyes and willed her body to ignore his hands.

'It's what it feels like if those rules of yours insist we never mix with people or go anywhere or have—what was it you called them? Oh, yeah—' his head turned '—PDA's... Put them all together and that sounds like hiding to me. And I'm not that guy who hides.'

Her heart twisted inside her chest as he continued.

'I'm that guy who enjoys his life—who goes for drinks, goes out to eat, goes on a sailing weekend with his mates to Galway and ends up at some dumb Oyster Festival...'

How did he *do* that? How did he make *her* feel guilty? Wasn't running around having great sex with no strings attached every guy's idea of heaven?

'And you're that kind of girl, Merrow. You know you are. I know you are. So by hiding we're, neither of us, being true to who we are. And that just doesn't sit well with me.'

And now she even ached because he'd stopped calling her *O'Connell*...

'Thing is, when you scratch an itch, the itch should go away, shouldn't it?'

His hands moved further up the backs of her legs, his thumbs brushing against her inner thighs and sending waves of heat to her very centre.

He didn't wait for an answer, continuing in a deep rumble that was just loud enough for her to hear as they stood in the quiet street.

'And it hasn't, has it?' His shoulders rose and fell again. 'If I walked the few feet it took to get us to the park outside my place and I set you down on the grass and undressed you and kissed you and touched you until you made all those noises you make when you're really turned on, are you telling me you'd want me to stop so you can go home?'

'No, I wouldn't want you to stop.' She couldn't lie to him about that.

Ever so slowly he tugged her forwards, letting her body slide down the hard length of his until her feet touched the pavement. Merrow shook her pony-tail into place and looked up into his eyes, his gorgeous hazel eyes with the gold flecks shining so bright and warm that looking into them turned her bones to mush. He smiled his half a smile, and reached his hands up to her face, smoothing loose strands of hair off her flushed cheeks with tender fingertips.

'So-o-o, we can stop doing this, which neither of us wants to do, or we can upgrade a little to more of a *public affair*. For however long it lasts.'

Merrow felt a smile tugging at the edges of her mouth. *'Upgrade?'*

'Yeah.' He nodded his head firmly, his smile growing as his fingertips finished smoothing hair and instead began tracing the sides of her face, trailing down along the line of her jaw and back up again. 'Nothing more complicated than that.'

It was already more complicated than that. But…

'I can cope with a very *small* upgrade, I suppose.'

'Good.' The smile was large enough to make her smile right on back, and then he jerked his head. 'C'mere.'

Merrow stepped in close and wrapped her arms around his neck, pressing her breasts in against his chest as his arms circled her waist. But instead of kissing her, he rocked her, shifting his weight from one foot to the other so that it was almost as if they were slow-dancing to some silent melody in his head. Then he pressed his lips against her hairline, against her temple, and whispered in her ear.

'See, that wasn't so hard, was it?'

It would be if she didn't keep her heart in check along the way. Entangling their lives more was a risky move, she knew that better than he probably did.

But she didn't say that; instead she grinned as the rocking from side to side changed to a rocking from side to side and moving forwards, so that she was being backed along the street towards his apartment.

'You really think you have me wrapped around your little finger, don't you?'

The burst of laughter vibrated his chest against her breasts and Merrow's eyelids grew heavy as she felt her nipples tauten.

'I'm working on it, O'Connell. But you're a challenge, I've gotta give you that.'

CHAPTER SIX

ALEX glanced at the clock readout on the bedside table just past Merrow's head. *Any minute now...*

She had this weird inner alarm clock built into her genetic code, and it was fairly reliable. Alex knew that, once he'd had time enough to study the pattern. And after almost a month he felt he had enough of that kind of knowledge to aim for another 'upgrade'.

His plan this time involved tiring her out better. Because he obviously wasn't doing that well enough when she still managed to wake after a short nap so she could get dressed and go home. Not once had she made the 'mistake' of staying all night. And frankly it was affecting Alex's allocated sleeping time, amongst other things...

Least, that was one of the reasons he was going to cite to her, *after* he did something about it.

She smiled in her sleep and he smiled in response.

Let's see what we can do about keeping that smile on your face...

Carefully, so he didn't let in a puff of cool air, he lifted the goose-feather duvet enough to give him some space. Then he propped his head on his hand so he could watch her face, his gaze straying over the rich auburn strands splayed over the pillow and beneath her cheek. Just once it would be nice to see that exact same picture as the damn sun came up outside.

He took a deep breath and held it, then oh-so-carefully ran the very tip of his fingertips along her arm from shoulder to wrist, while he exhaled as quietly as he could manage.

She sighed in her sleep.

Stay asleep just a while longer…

He whispered his fingertips across to the jut of her hipbone, tracing it in a slow circle before he turned his hand over and whispered his knuckles over the inward curve of her waist. She had a *great* body. All dips and curves. And he knew every single inch of that body now, had mentally mapped it out onto his memory.

When his knuckles brushed the even softer skin at the side of her breast she murmured, her lips parting.

Shh. Wait.

Turning his hand again he traced under her breast, following the heavier curve all the way round and up to her sternum, then back down again before turning his hand to graze his knuckles over her nipple. He felt it respond, gradually peaking beneath his touch. Even in her sleep she responded to him.

'*Mmm…*'

The low sound had an immediate effect on his own body, and he tightened the muscles of his thighs, closing his eyes briefly to concentrate on slowing down his response while he continued to tease her breast.

But the thought of what was to come, of pushing deep inside her and feeling her flex around the hard length of him, was too tempting an image to fight. It was what he intended doing, after all.

She just needed to stay in that half-asleep dreamlike state for a little longer.

He moved his hand back and forth and back and forth, slowly, gently, turning it back into more of a soothing touch, meant to lull her back into a deeper sleep again.

And when her breathing evened out, only then did he move his hand down, dipping in where her belly button created a valley, rising over the gentle, tiny rise of her lower abdomen, brushing his knuckles over the very tips of the curled hair between her thighs.

'*Alex...*' She exhaled his name on so low a whisper he barely heard it. Was she dreaming about him touching her? Fantasising about him making love to her while she remained pliant and willing him on without uttering words of encouragement as she usually did?

He thought it was the most erotic thought of his life, and his fingertips gently eased her soft thighs apart...

Merrow was having the most erotic dream of her life.

She was caught up in that mystical area between deep sleep and waking up, where dreams were filled with shadowy images, where imagined touches made her skin tingle with a sensitivity she'd never quite felt when she was fully awake. Oh, and it felt *so-o-o* good...

'*Yes...*' She could feel her legs being gently eased further apart, could feel the whispering sensation of fingertips seeking her opening.

In her dream she was so moist already, her body weeping with need for the touch to move deeper, to tease her, taunt her, to coax her to the brink of an abyss she would tumble into with complete heavenly abandon.

The touch met moisture, traced her folds, parting her, opening her for more gentle exploration. *So good...don't stop...don't...*

'Don't stop…'

Her invisible dream lover exhaled, the air tickling her naked shoulder. And she turned her face towards the source, ran the tip of her tongue over her dry lips, moaning softly as one long finger slid inside her.

'So good…'

A battle started inside her foggy mind between remaining in the beautiful dream or opening her eyes to look at the man the more awake part of her brain knew was lying beside her. But she hung on to the dream, reaching for it with invisible hands, for just a little while longer…

The long finger moved in and out, and she arched her hips up into his touch every time he pushed back in. No one had ever made her feel this amazing. Surely it had to be a dream? And if it was a dream she really didn't want to leave it. In fact, the very thought of leaving it twisted her heart in her chest, tearing a small sob from her lips.

'Shh.' The whisper moved her hair against her heated cheek. 'I'm here.'

Alex. Had she said his name? She didn't know. She was so close already, could feel the knot of tension tightening, could feel the heat coiling low in her abdomen, her inner muscles drawing his finger in deeper.

One finger became two, stretching her wider, drawing another, more distinctly guttural moan from the base of her throat as she pushed her head back deeper into the deep pillows.

'Alex…'

She could feel herself being drawn into the reality of it, away from the ache in her chest that had thought it was just a dream.

'I'm here,' he whispered into her ear this time as she drew shorter, deeper breaths. 'Keep your eyes closed. Keep dreaming.'

She arched her spine up off the mattress, felt his fingers move, turn, stretch her, filling her up. And her breathing got faster with each gentle move. This wasn't just an itch being scratched, wasn't just sex. This was Alex making love to her, worshipping her body with his touch, making her feel so, *so* wonderful.

Oh, she was *so* close.

'*Please*—' She'd never begged in her life. Not once.

'Tell me what you want.'

'*You*. I want *you*. *Please*.' She couldn't get enough air into her lungs, her throat aching from gasping so hard. But still he held her on the edge, so she felt as if she were trying to balance on a taut, *tight* rope hundreds of miles above the earth.

'I'm right here.' His warm lips placed butterfly-soft kisses along the side of her arched neck, drawing more soft sighs and low moans from her lips as every nerve ending in her body seemed to be drawing her upwards, striving for something that was just out of reach, no matter how hard she strained to touch it…

Her lover teased her clitoris with a single stroke and her whole body jerked. *Her lover.* And whether asleep and dreaming or awake and living the dream, she knew he lived up to that title more than any mere 'boyfriend' ever had.

It was achingly too *right*, too *perfect* again.

Another frustrated sob moved up her throat from her aching chest. '*Alex*—'

'I've got you.' He thumbed moisture over her clitoris again and she fell apart, her spine arching up like a bow-string as she rode the waves, clamping her thighs tight around his hand to hold on to the sensation for as long as she could.

'*Oh*—'

She convulsed around his fingers.

'*My*—'

Her hips bucked again.

'*God*—'

She panted out the last word and fell back onto the mattress, every inch of her body pulsing with waves from the aftershock of the most powerful orgasm she'd ever experienced—ever—and maybe ever would again.

She could have wept when his fingers slipped free. How did he *do* that to her? When had she handed over *complete possession* of her body to him?

A deep, rumbling chuckle vibrated in her ear. 'And we're just getting started.'

He honestly thought she had anything left after *that*?

'I don't think I can do that again.'

'Yes, you can.'

No, really, she couldn't. And she still hadn't got round to opening her eyes yet!

She'd open them in a minute. When her body had stopped convulsing, when her heart rate had slowed down, when she could *breathe*, when she could actually uncurl her toes again, for crying out loud! If they stayed that way she'd never be able to wear shoes again.

'Did you have a nice dream?' his deep husky voice asked into her ear. 'Was it a sexy dream?'

Sexy didn't begin to cover it. 'Mmm-hmm.'

She pursed her dry lips tight together, and then damped them again. It was almost unbearably warm—sweltering hot, in fact—so she kicked the duvet off her legs and Alex helped by throwing the rest of it back off both their bodies.

Then his weight shifted, and she felt him move something beside her head. If she'd had the energy to open her heavy eyelids then she might have been able to see what he was doing. But it would have to wait a minute. Just another wee minute.

She should write to *Cosmo* about this one.

The bed moved a little, the blissfully cooler air surrounding her shifted, then her body was rolled a little towards him as the mattress dipped and, overly sensitised, she jumped when his large hand cupped her hip.

'Lift up for me.'

That got her eyes open. And she tilted her chin down to find him kneeling between the legs he was coaxing apart. 'What are you doing *now*?'

He smiled a sinfully wicked smile at her. 'I'm picking up where your dream left off.'

'You have *got* to be kidding me!'

When she didn't lift her hips, he set both hands on them and lifted her, kneeing what she could now see was a pillow beneath her, so that her pelvis was tilted up. And she groaned, because she knew he could get a deeper angle that way.

'Are you trying to kill me? I thought you liked me.'

'I'm demonstrating how much I like you. Sometimes actions speak louder than words...' He lifted her heavy legs and wrapped them around his waist and Merrow used every ounce of strength she had left to lock her ankles, despite her continuing vocal protests.

'Seriously, are you *on* something, you know, some kind of drug enhancing—?' She cried out as he filled her with one long thrust. *'Oh!'*

He chuckled as he leaned in for a languid kiss, his words rumbling against her lips while the vibration of his chuckle reverberated inside her. 'Nope. This is all me.'

He slid out, almost leaving her before he thrust forward to emphasise the word 'me'.

The muscles in his arms strained, his elbows bent as he held his full weight off her body and kissed her again.

'You *see*—' his hips flexed back, and forwards a little

harder '—I've *noticed*—' and back, and forwards a little harder again '—I don't seem *to be*—' and again '—satisfying *you enough*—' and again '—so I *aim*—' again '—to *fix that*.'

'You don't—oh—' she felt the knot of tension build again '—you don't think—mmm…' Her hands rose to grip hold of his biceps, his arms wobbling when her fingernails dug into his skin so that she knew the kind of self-control he was exerting. 'How can you think—I'm—oh-h-h—not—Alex—?'

When he kissed her again, suckling on her bottom lip, running his tongue along the inside of her upper teeth, he slowed the pace, and the angle the pillow had raised her into, combined with the pressure of his hard pelvis rocking against her already tender bundle of nerve endings, threw her into another sudden, shockingly deep orgasm.

'Alex!' She groaned against his mouth when he continued moving, making the ripples last longer. 'You're going to have to call an ambulance for me. How can you think for one second—?'

He kissed her slowly, softer this time, nibbling on her lower lip and looking down at her with a gaze that made her shudder with a wave of what briefly felt like fear again,

'You keep running out on me, O'Connell.'

She swallowed hard.

He flexed his hips back, then forwards. 'You never stay. I can't be tiring you out enough.'

So this was his answer? He was going to leave her so completely sexually exhausted that she'd have no choice but to fall asleep in his arms, and stay that way, his body tangled with hers until she eventually woke up beside him?

Even as he straightened out his arms, his chest lifting to let a whisper of cool air brush over her highly sensitised breasts, she still felt as if her chest were being crushed. He was using the best sex of her life to get her to participate in something she viewed as way more dangerous than the best sex of her life.

If she stayed—

He increased the tempo and her breathing sped up again, even as she frowned up at the tightening cords in his neck.

If she let him *hold her* all night—

Her vision blurred as she saw his jaw clench, as she felt him increase the pressure again, changing the angle of his thrust so that he was once again grinding against her most sensitive place, forcing her headlong into another cataclysmic explosion.

If he started to take as strong a hold over her heart as he already held over her body—

She arched upwards and closed her eyes tight, her teeth biting her bottom lip hard enough to have drawn blood, her fingers sliding down his arms to grasp on his large hands flat against the sheets. And she felt the blood burn through her veins as he went still, his hard length pulsing inside her while bright sparks of light exploded like fireworks behind her clamped eyelids.

If he made her *fall* for him—

She lay very still for a long, long while, her body humming as she fought for some control over the wave of emotion consuming her. She couldn't let it happen. She wouldn't let it happen. 'Perfect' never lasted, did it?

'O'Connell, look at me.'

She pursed her lips together to get the feeling back into the now swollen lip she had bitten down so hard on. And she took a deep, shuddering breath before she dared to open her eyes and look up at his face.

He was still breathing hard. He had short tendrils of blond hair sticking to the sheen of perspiration on his forehead. But he was studying her with a small frown on his face.

While she continued to stare back, he rested his weight on one elbow, and leaned his upper body closer, lifting his other hand to thumb moisture from the corner of her eye. And he frowned harder as his eyes studied it, rubbing it between his thumb and forefinger.

Then he looked back into her eyes. 'Did I just hurt you? Was I in too deep?'

'No.' She grimaced inwardly at his choice of words, but pinned a smile in place and tried to lighten the moment. 'Though I might just need that ambulance now.'

But Alex didn't smile back, his eyes narrowing. He searched her eyes, leaned away a little and broke the bond between their lower bodies before moving back to her side, turning over to reach for the duvet, and covering their bodies before he propped his elbow and rested his head on his hand.

Merrow prayed for the strength to bluff her way through, turning her head on the pillow to look up at him, raising her eyebrows.

'You didn't hurt me, Alex, I promise. And for the record, I've *never* been so satisfied—*seriously*. Any man who can make a woman weep with pleasure should feel pretty damn proud of himself.'

The frown softened, but a look of suspicion remained in his eyes. 'If that's the only reason then I'd *be* pretty proud of myself.'

'It is.' It was the first time she'd lied outright to him. And *that* hurt.

'I'm not so sure.' He reached out to do his usual brushing-back of hair off her cheek, his deep voice low and heartbreak-ingly persuasive. 'What is it you're so scared of, O'Connell?'

This. It would have been the honest answer. But instead she lied to him again, the cramp in her chest increasing with each lie. 'I'm not scared.'

She rolled onto her side, lifting her hand to his face, as if the fact she wasn't afraid to reach for him were some kind of reassurance she was telling him the truth. Her palm cupped his square jaw, the tip of her thumb fitted perfectly into the dimple in his chin. And her gaze softened; he really was a very beautiful man, wasn't he? Yes, he carried the confidence that came with knowing that, because how could he *not* know how he looked? But he never abused the gift; arrogant on occasion, yes—cocky, without a doubt—but never as much of an ass as he could have been if he'd been vain.

It was an element of his danger…

His hand slid down to her neck, fingers tangling in her hair. 'So what excuse do I get tonight? I know you don't have an early meeting with a client, 'cos you're working with me tomorrow. I know you're not meeting the rest of the musketeers for breakfast, 'cos we're meeting Mickey D for coffee. You can't have laundry again, 'cos you've done laundry at least three times this week already. So what's going to get you out of my bed this time? When it would make much more sense for you to stay over the odd night, to throw a toothbrush into your bag, or some of that tiny excuse for underwear— neither of which would take up that much room in your bag realistically…'

A toothbrush, fresh underwear, and then she'd be keeping a change of clothes here, would have a drawer of her own in one of the massive dresser drawers on the far side of the room. She'd have products lined up on the shelves in the bathroom beside his pathetically male lack of *stuff*…

Tangled. She'd be letting her life get even more tangled up in his, like weaving the threads into a tapestry where the pattern would never quite work.

'I have Fred to think of.'

'You can't hide behind a goldfish. It's a physical impossibility.'

'With any pet comes responsibility. And I already killed Wilma.'

'Maybe it was just Wilma's time to go. Now she's swimming in the great toilet bowl in the sky…'

She laughed when he chuckled at his own joke. 'You're mean.'

'No, *you're* mean.' He sidled a little closer to her, the heat building between their bodies beneath the heavy duvet as he looked into her eyes with an intense gaze. 'You know I haven't slept right one single night since we started this?'

Her eyes widened in surprise. 'You haven't?'

'Nope.' He shook his head against her hand, and aimed a petulant-little-boy look at her that made her smile again. 'You wreak havoc with my sleep pattern. You tire me out, then we get all snuggled in and the next thing I know you're waking me up to skip across town and check your place didn't catch fire while you were gone. Then when I stay awake long enough to know you're hopefully home in one piece and I finally get back to sleep, I wake up horny in the morning with no one here to help me do anything about it. That's *mean*.'

She giggled, her heart warming at the thought of him worrying she'd got home while her head knew she shouldn't allow herself to get sucked in by his sob story. 'Poor, poor neglected child.'

He nodded when she moved her hand off his face, cradling the back of his head as she sidled in closer and lifted her leg over his. 'Yup. Why do you think I insist on so many *brunches*?'

'I *love* brunch.' She massaged her fingers against the short coarse hair at the back of his head, and watched as his eyes grew heavy.

'What does it say in your affair handbook about mistresses and sleep-overs with their playboy lovers?'

She weighed up the pros and cons of that for a while, until his thick lashes rose and he looked into her eyes again. He didn't say a word. He just looked at her for a long while, and then the corners of his mouth lifted into the hint of a smile she loved so much.

And she was done for. 'It says that maybe the mistress should try it once just to see. But the playboy lover shouldn't take it to mean that the mistress doesn't still have her own life.'

The hand on her neck moved, slid between their bodies and wrapped around her waist to tug her closer, his chin resting on the top of her head when she nestled in against his shoulder. 'You see; I'm okay with that.'

'You hog the duvet and I'm gone.'

'You go and I promise you you'll miss the best wake-up call of your year.'

She lay still for a long while, her fingers still massaging his scalp while she listened to him breathing, how the breaths evened out, growing deeper as he surrendered to sleep. And her heart ached again.

She needed her head examined.

What was she doing? Why could she never seem to resist when he set his mind to persuading her to do what he wanted? First it had been mixing with each other's friends and PDAs, and now he had her sleeping over—his face the last thing before she surrendered to sleep, where she would spend the night in his arms, and when she woke up, his face would be the first thing she saw.

He didn't want anything serious any more than she did. So why did he keep pushing the boundaries?

She turned around, as if somehow facing away from him

would give her a little more distance. But he simply grumbled and pulled her back against him, his arm a possessive weight around her waist.

If he could just stop being so much more than she needed him to be at this point in her life, if he could just be—*less perfect*...

Alex grumbled again behind her, then rolled away to flick off the light switch before pulling her back into place. And Merrow lay very still, blinking into the darkness, waiting for his breathing to even out again.

'Stop thinking about it and go to sleep, O'Connell.'

Damn! How did he *know* that? Sometimes he could be such a—

'And stop calling me names in your head. I can hear you.'

She scowled into the darkness. But eventually the sound of his breathing and the steady beat of his heart against her back began to lull her into an irresistible sense of security. Because, all things considered, he really had done a very good job of tiring her out.

She just needed to remember not to rely on that sense of security. She needed to not feel so safe held in his arms. She needed to think about not caving in every single time he set his mind to persuading her to—

But sleep crept in and her thoughts went fuzzy.

CHAPTER SEVEN

'Oh I dunno. I liked the fuchsia one.'

'Too pink with auburn hair.'

'The gold one was sexy.'

'Get away with you. She looked like an Oscars statue in it.'

Merrow let the debate continue as she flicked through the racks of clothes in her favourite vintage clothing store. Normally a day with her friends trawling the shops and sipping foamy coffees as they watched the world go by was her idea of heaven.

But she'd had her visions of heaven altered some of late. And she couldn't remember ever feeling that one damn dress was so important before!

If Alex had ruined *shopping* for her there would be hell to pay…

'What about this one?' Lisa held a blue seventies off-the-shoulder number up in front of her body.

But Merrow merely shrugged silently. It wasn't 'the one'. And the dress they found would just jump straight out and announce itself as 'the one', she felt. It would have to be that special. Because she'd never actually been to a party with the equivalent of Irish royalty before and she needed every confidence booster she could find, thanks anyway.

Lisa lowered the dress and studied her profile when she went back to the racks. 'Okay, what's up?'

'There's nothing up.'

'There's something up. Did you have a row with Alex?'

'No.' She sighed as the others crowded in. 'I did *not* have a row with Alex.'

Gracie laid a hand on her arm. 'If you tell us he pulled a Dylan we'll all go round his house and help you cut up his clothes into tiny wee pieces.'

Her mouth twitched at the thought. It was what they *should* have done with Dylan, but they hadn't thought about it till afterwards, when they'd downed a large bottle of champagne to celebrate his 'demise' and made a list of the things they 'could' have done to get him back for his dastardly deeds. Somehow, she suspected if Alex ever did anything to merit their equivalent of 'just desserts' his wardrobe loss would prove much more expensive than Dylan's ever would have.

'No, he didn't pull a Dylan.'

'Better not think about it either. Where did you say he was this weekend? It's not Galway again, right?'

Ouch. Well, no, it wasn't Galway, but planting that idea in her head didn't help. It was the first weekend they'd spent apart in coming up on six weeks, and Merrow hated that she missed him so much. That was what she got for getting into the routine of staying at his place on a Friday and Saturday night—to say nothing of the night or two midweek. She even had a toothbrush and a change of clothes there, *already*.

'He's up north somewhere racing sail-boats. He'll be back tomorrow night.'

'I thought there had to be a reason for that tan. Sailing makes sense.' Lou moved in and wrapped an arm around her shoulders. 'You miss him, that's all. You'll be grand when he's home.'

Hell, even the musketeers were seeing them as a couple now. She rolled her eyes, and now she thought of them as *the musketeers* too! That was Alex's doing—again. Damn him to hell in a handbag. A very *small* handbag. And not even a *nice* handbag.

'Listen to Lou, she knows what she's talking about.' Gracie's blonde head bobbed.

Yes, because as the only married one amongst them that automatically made Lou the fountain of all knowledge when it came to relationships. Well, it was Lou's fault they'd been in Galway in the first place—it had been *her* hen weekend— so, as far as Merrow was concerned, it was partly *her* fault she was in her current predicament.

Lisa parted the clothing on the rail and inserted the blue dress at random. 'We don't blame you for falling for him. He's *yum*.'

There were nods of agreement.

'There's no point in me falling for him,' she mumbled in reply as she moved out of Lou's embrace towards a dress peeking out at her near the end of the rack. 'An O'Connell isn't going to end up playing happily ever after with a Fitzgerald.'

'Oh, you did *not* just say that!'

Crap. She needed to complain more quietly next time. These three never missed a thing.

'Why doesn't an O'Connell end up with a Fitzgerald? And don't you dare say you think you're not good enough for him!'

'I don't think that. It's got nothing to do with him and me.'

'Well, who does it have something to do with, then, if it's not you two? How many people are in this relationship with you?'

'It's not a relationship. It's just sex.' But that was yet another lie, wasn't it? She was getting good at this lying lark. Or not. 'Rubbish.'

'*Look—*' dropping her hand from the edge of the material that had caught her eye, she swung round to face her friends '—you guys know me and you've all met my family. Do you really see my lot mixing in with the Fitzgerald dynasty? And no matter what any of you say, you can't deny that any "relationship" at some point involves families mixing together. It can't be avoided.'

They stared at her for a stunned silent minute. It was the tone of her voice that had probably done it. Because Merrow knew there had been an edge of desperation in there. She just desperately needed *someone* to understand why she was struggling so badly of late. *Anyone.*

Just *one* of them then, *dammit*!

Lisa, ever the brutally honest one of them, tilted her head and crinkled her nose as she examined the ceiling. 'You gotta admit that would make for an interesting wedding day.'

'*See!*' She raised her arm and dropped it to her side, exhaling with relief that finally *someone* could see her point of view. 'I can just see my mum with Arthur Fitzgerald—he could chat about winning international awards for architecture, and she could give him some tips on the art of tantric yoga.'

There was a snigger from the cheap seats, which was cut off by an elbow swiftly poked into ribs before Lisa stepped closer. 'Hon, it mightn't be all that bad. Interesting definitely, but maybe not as bad as you think it'd be...'

Oh, she was so not contemplating *a wedding day* with Alex now! This had to stop! She rolled her eyes, shook her head and turned away, her gaze skimming the rack. Where was that dress again?

'You're just worried about meeting his parents, that's all. Can't say I blame you...'

'I'm not worried about meeting them. I meet people all the

time. If I'm worried about anything it's that they'll be as great as he is.'

'Yes, I can see how that would be a worry.' She followed Merrow as she rediscovered the dress that had called to her from half a rack away. 'You know, I don't think I've ever seen you so sideways before, not even when you found out about Dylan. I know it maybe doesn't feel so great right this minute, but, for what it's worth, I think he's *perfect* for you.'

'Yeah.' She walked to the long mirror and held the dress up in front of her. It was *the one*, without a doubt. Her eyes met Lisa's in the reflection and she smiled a small, sad smile. 'That's exactly the problem.'

Alex wandered to the end of the jetty and fished his mobile out of his pocket, turning it end over end in his palm as he looked out over the water and contemplated calling her.

Funny, he'd never hesitated on so simple a decision before. There wasn't that much to it. All he had to do was flip open the cover and hit a button or two. And then there was the added incentive of her famous sexy phone voice on the other end…

But was calling her when he was only away for a couple of nights breaking one of her ridiculous rules?

He was already pushing the limits on those and he knew he was. Thing was, he couldn't seem to remove the memory of those few tears she'd shed the last time he'd pushed the boundaries. So he hadn't pushed since.

Even when he'd really wanted to.

It was the most strategic game of cat and mouse he'd ever played before. But someone as free-spirited, as confident, as full of life as Merrow O'Connell might just be one of the few women who would truly hate the lifestyle of a Fitzgerald. Being a Fitzgerald came with certain responsibilities, a sense of duty; it meant living under scrutiny a lot of the time. And she'd hate all that, wouldn't she? He didn't want to be the one to attempt to clip her wings.

But, man, could she ever shake his family up.

He smiled out at the water. She'd already shaken *his* life. It was almost worth putting on a suit these days just to have her make moves to loosen him up. And to think he'd thought he had a pretty damn full and fulfilling life *before* he'd met her. Now his life just seemed—*richer*, somehow, didn't it?

And he missed her. He'd bet that wasn't allowed either. Well, tough. He did.

So he flipped the phone open and hit a couple of buttons. Because he reckoned that was what playboy lovers probably did when they wanted to talk to a mistress they missed having around.

'Hey, Captain. Or should that be "Ahoy, Captain"?'

He chuckled at her greeting. '*Funny*—you out with the musketeers?'

'Yes, I am, indeed. We shopped 'til we dropped and then we had something to eat and now we're off out for the night. Lisa says we're gonna make some mischief.'

Alex wandered along the wooden boards, the pontoon-like jetty moving beneath his deck shoes. 'What kind of mischief, exactly?'

'Ah-h-h…now that would be telling…'

He felt a sudden wave of possessiveness, thinking of that first night he'd met her when she'd been out 'making mischief' with the rest of the musketeers. But he swallowed the emotion down. He doubted she'd appreciate him being possessive either—another rule broken.

There was a call from the other end of the jetty. 'Hey, Alex! Pint?'

Alex nodded, lifting his phone from his ear to call back. 'You get this one. I'll get the next.'

When he set the phone back to his ear, the familiar sexy voice crooned, 'And it would seem I'm not the only one off out to make mischief…'

'The yacht club is putting on a do for the visiting crews. It'll probably be a late night. So I thought I'd check up on you now while I can still dial.'

There was a very brief pause, but it was enough to bring another smile to his face when her voice changed to the brighter tone she usually used to cover something up. 'Well, have fun. I've prior knowledge of those wild sailing weekends away from home.'

'You have nothing to worry about.'

'You don't have to say that to me, Alex.'

'I think I do.'

When there was another pause, he stopped walking, straining to hear her breathing on the other end of the line before he dropped his voice a little. 'I'm not Dylan.'

'I know that. And, for the record, Dylan wasn't as big a deal as you seem to think he was.'

He wasn't? A part of Alex was pleased to hear that, but another part was vaguely confused by it. He'd thought a broken heart from a cheating boyfriend was the main reason she'd so much difficulty trusting this time round. And if that wasn't the reason, then what was? The question left a frown on his face.

'What was he, then?'

'A mistake.'

Obviously. 'But he did cheat on you.'

She sighed. 'Yes, he did. Every time he went away with his football pals for the weekend, as it happens, while I played house. So there you go, you have all the gory details now.'

'Well, then, he's still a loser.' Suddenly something else made sense. 'You lived together?'

'Yes. And we're done talking about this now.'

Well, that might explain some of the initial problems with sleepovers. He should talk to her on the phone more often if it got him this much information in one go, but the bigger picture also pushed him into crossing the line with her again.

'O'Connell?'

'Yes?'

'Tell me you know I'm not going to cheat on you.'

'Alex—' His name came out on a soft edge of warning.

''Cos we playboy lovers tend to stick with the one mistress at a time, you know—especially when that one mistress is more than enough to keep us occupied.'

She grumbled back at him. 'I'm not there to keep you occupied. I'm here with no one to tire me out.'

'Does that mean you miss me?'

'Like a hole in the head.'

'Liar.'

She laughed, low and sexy, and his body stiffened in response. 'When are you back?'

''Bout eight tomorrow night—maybe a little later. I'll come to your place and you can introduce me to Fred.'

'You'll hate my place. Why don't you just call me when you're home and I'll come to yours?'

'You don't know I'll hate your place. You're just worried I might get to know you better by seeing it.'

'You know enough about me already. It's got nothing to do with that. You're an architect, you like good design. My place will do your head in.'

'How about you let me be the judge of that?'

'Alex, if I know you're coming to my place I'll feel the

need to do things like clean up, wash dishes and actually use a vacuum cleaner. I'll be wrecked by the time you get here. Trust me. Highly organised isn't in my genetic make-up. I have an *artistic nature*...'

Alex thought the lady did protest too much. 'It won't be your apartment I'm there to see. And so long as there's a bed we'll be fine. There'll be catching up to do. I'll even bring take-out we can microwave later, to keep our strength up.' He paused. 'Tell me you have a microwave.'

'Yes, I have a microwave.'

There was another long silence, and Alex knew she was trying to decide whether or not to let him into yet another corner of her life. It wasn't so easy to persuade her to change her mind when he couldn't use his usual methods, was it?

'Then I'll call you when we have the boat stowed away and you can tell me how to get there.'

More silence.

So he pushed again, using his most persuasive tone. 'You know me by now. I want to see you. And if that means I have to drive to the office to look up your address and sit on your doorstep with take-out going cold until you take pity on me and open the door, then you know that's exactly what I'll do. So just give in now and save us both some time.'

'You can be a real pain sometimes.'

'See, I told you you knew me.'

He waited again, ruing the fact that he could practically hear her foot tapping while she thought and yet he wasn't there to kiss the frown off her face until she caved in.

'There are a gazillion unknowns in take-out. I'll make something for us.'

'That works for me.' He grinned broadly, possessed by a sudden need to punch the air in victory. 'Just don't go making so much mischief with the musketeers that I have to go the garda station to bail you out.'

'Ha, ha.' He heard reluctant amusement in her voice.

'O'Connell?'

'Yes, Alex.' He heard resignation this time.

'I miss you too.'

'Are these your parents?'

Merrow cringed as she tossed the ingredients for a Greek salad into a bowl. He'd kissed her breathless the second he'd arrived, the taste of sea salt still on his lips, but the second she'd pulled away to see to the food he'd started prowling her apartment. Not that it would take that long, realistically, for him to walk from one side of it to the other when the entire place could probably have fitted into his three or four times.

But her entire life was fitted inside the compact space, and the fact that he was studying every knick-knack, every book spine and every photograph with so much interest was making her nervous.

She glanced over to see which picture he had in his hands. 'Yes, that's them.'

'What age are you in this?'

'Am I wearing bright green dungarees?'

'Excruciatingly bright green dungarees, with what looks like a pink T-shirt. Thank God you have better colour coordination now.'

'At six that kind of combination is fun.' In theory—her friends at school had had several other words to use to describe it back in the day. But after a few years they'd got used to it.

'Is this a holiday cabin somewhere?'

She sighed. 'No, that's where we lived. They still live there. It's a bit bigger now, though.'

She glanced across again and saw his brows quirk the tiniest amount in surprise. Well, she had said that their two worlds were very different.

'Where is it?'

'On the Dingle Peninsula.' She focussed on the salad, cubing feta cheese and adding it to the mix. 'The less touristy side.'

'What do they do?'

Dammit. He just would ask, wouldn't he? It wasn't that she was ashamed of her parents, because she wasn't. If it weren't for them she wouldn't be the strong-minded, free-willed, confident individual she was as an adult. She knew that. But standing telling a Fitzgerald what they did, even if it *was* Alex, brought back memories of her awkward teenage years. When, on top of coping with things like puberty and peer pressure, Merrow had also had to cope with the embarrassment factor of her parents' 'work'.

She cleared her throat and used the stock answer from those years. 'They run a kind of holiday centre.'

She glanced over and saw Alex replace the frame on the shelf, his gaze moving to the next one, leaning forwards to study it closer.

'It's a good spot for water sports over there—great windsurfing.'

If only! That way she'd have actually had something else in common with him. But, oh, no…

'Okay, holiday centre is maybe misleading…' She tilted her head back and tried to remember some of the other descriptions she'd once used to avoid laying it all on the line. '*Retreat* might be a better word…'

Alex turned round and looked at her with an expression of amused curiosity. 'Now I'm intrigued.'

She pursed her lips together, frowning down at the salad

as she sprinkled on sliced black olives. 'I did tell you never the twain when it came to our worlds.'

'And I've never quite understood what that meant. So how about you explain it to me?'

She glanced at him again from beneath her long lashes, damping her lips with the end of her tongue. It would be so much easier to drive the beginnings of a wedge between them if he weren't standing there looking so delicious.

Dressed in faded jeans and a short-sleeved polo shirt of a darker blue, with the short spikes of his blond hair a little more blond and his tan just a little deeper from his weekend on the waves, he was heart-wrenchingly gorgeous. And she really, *really* had missed him.

Her stupid heart had even jumped when she saw him.

And now she was about to point out the monumental distance between their two families. If he was weird about it, then she'd have to call him on being a snob. If he made one of the raucous jokes that her teenage peers had made, she'd hate him a little for it. But either way, it would be the beginning of the end.

His dark blond brows rose again.

So she took a deep breath and dived on in. 'They run a sex therapy retreat. Couples go there to learn meditation, yoga, massage techniques, stuff like that. And my mother is a Tantra Master.'

Then she waited.

Alex's expression didn't change. So she waited some more. But when she was just about ready to lift her lovely Greek salad and throw it at him, he nodded slowly and said, 'Okay.'

Her eyes narrowed. 'Okay? That's all you're going to say?'

'I might need a minute with this.'

She *knew* it! Of course he was going to need a bloody

minute. Even now he was painting a very vivid picture in his mind about the way she'd been raised and about her family, wasn't he? And he would then move on to realising how far apart their two backgrounds were. It would only take a heart-beat or two after that for him to realise why this whole 'playing at being a couple' thing they were doing was completely pointless. Then maybe he'd see why an affair was the best and only option.

Which would mean he'd see she'd been right all along—so why didn't it feel good to know that?

'To be honest my mind went a bit blank after you mentioned sex therapy.' When she pursed her lips again he smiled. 'Because I was thinking it's not like we need any of that…'

'I wasn't suggesting we booked in.'

He reached a hand out and stole an olive off her chopping board, continuing while chewing. 'Some of the other stuff sounded like it had possibilities, though. Tell me more.'

What? She stared at him with wide eyes. And caught the spark of gold just before his gaze lowered and he stole another olive. Hang on a minute—

'Oh-h-h, you've got to be kidding. You're getting *turned on* by this?'

'O'Connell, I've been turned on since I got in the car to come here. This conversation is just adding to it, is all. My imagination is running riot. And you like it when I get creative.'

Merrow was flabbergasted. 'None of this bothers you?'

He looked back into her eyes. 'Why would it? If anything it explains why you don't have as many hang-ups as some women do about sex. With parents like yours you've probably been encouraged to talk about everything and anything and that'll be part of the reason you're as confident as you are. Remind me to thank them for that when I meet them.'

When he met them?

He leaned forwards a little, his voice dropping. 'Now tell me more about the massage techniques…'

'Alex, I'm not taking you to meet my parents.'

'I'm not suggesting we jump in the car *now*.'

'It's never, *ever* going to happen.'

He stood tall again, and Merrow saw something cross his eyes. He even avoided her gaze. And combined with the way his body language had changed she knew something was very wrong, so she backtracked in an attempt to get them back to where they'd been when he'd walked in the door.

She walked round the counter and set her hand on his bent elbow, turning him round to face her. 'Playboy lovers don't go to meet their mistress's parents.'

'That's another rule from the handbook, is it?'

'Yes, that it most definitely is.' She wrapped her arms around his lean waist and stepped in closer, tilting her chin to look up at him. 'But I *can* do something about the massage techniques.'

The fact that he didn't try to touch her sent a tremor of fear up her spine. Instead he studied her face for a long time, intently, as if he was trying to make up his mind whether to say whatever was on his mind.

And she was almost afraid to ask. Instead she smiled a small smile and quirked her brows.

His eyes narrowed. 'How long are we playing this game for?'

Merrow swallowed hard, her smile fading. 'What game?'

'The game where we pretend there's nothing going on here—' he glanced briefly over her head '—when we both know this isn't just about sex.'

She stepped back from him.

'And there she goes again, backing away.' He shook his

head and looked at her with an expression that translated to her as disappointment. 'I don't get it. I thought you were holding back because your last boyfriend hurt you badly by cheating on you. But on the phone you told me it wasn't that big a deal.'

'It wasn't.' And the fact that he'd used the term '*last* boyfriend' again didn't escape her. But she already felt as if they were on dangerous enough ground so she let it go, again. 'I wasn't enough in love with him for him to have broken my heart. I was just…disappointed in him. Maybe a little humiliated that I hadn't seen the signs, but nothing more than that.'

Alex nodded, his lips a thin line before he answered with a gruff, 'And, you see, even now the look on your face is telling me you didn't want me to know that.'

Because she hadn't, that was why. What woman was happy explaining to any man the disasters that preceded him? Especially the kind of man who had probably never had anyone cheat on him? Who *would*?

'Because it has nothing to do with this.'

'Well, do you mind telling me what it is that's getting in the way, then? 'Cos there's *something*.'

Merrow didn't know what to say or do—for the first time in a long time—but then she'd never met anyone as dangerous as Alex before. If she let him in, *really* let him in, then he'd have the ability to hurt her on a level she'd never let herself be hurt before. But she couldn't brush it over by making love with him this time. Not when he was already so distant. And that already hurt on a whole new level, her heart feeling as if it were being crushed tight in her chest.

Her hesitation made Alex frown all the harder. 'Well, maybe when you want to tell me what it is you'll let me know. You know where I am.'

Merrow watched in astonishment as he lifted his jacket off the back of her sofa, holding it so tight in his fist that his knuckles went white. He was *leaving*?

'I thought we both agreed we didn't want anything serious at this point in our lives?'

He turned round at the door, tilting his head to an angle that added to the sarcastic tone in his voice. 'When we agreed to all your hidden rules?'

'Alex—'

His deep voice dropped a level, held a husky edge that suggested he was holding back a lot more than he was throwing at her. 'It might have been better if I'd been given a copy of those rules at the start. Then it wouldn't feel like I'm constantly trying to dance my way round them.'

He shook his head again, ran a hand over his face. 'I'm tired, O'Connell—I've been driving for hours. And I'm tired of playing a game I don't know the rules for. That's all. Like I said—you know where I am.'

CHAPTER EIGHT

MERROW put him through five days of hell. Well, it felt like it. One of the most maddening things being the fact that even his pre-Merrow version of days filled to the full just weren't enough any more.

It meant by the time she appeared at the Pavenham for their weekly meeting with Mickey D he had to call on every iota of his social training as a Fitzgerald to keep his cool.

He shook hands with Mickey and invited Merrow to lay her sketches out on the new reception desk alongside the photos and plans he'd already set out. And then he went through his update with his voice calm, his demeanour businesslike, and without looking at her once.

Because the one look when she'd arrived had been enough. Thanks anyway.

It wasn't that she'd chosen to wear one of the short skirts that made him insane—oh, no. She'd played it smarter than that. She had on a perfectly demure pale gold, round-necked blouse that just happened to show a glimpse of flat midriff every time she moved, and hip-hugging cropped trousers that adoringly covered her long legs and gave a nice view of each shapely calf—shown to best effect by the impractical high-heeled strappy shoes that ended with peep toes painted the same pale gold as her blouse.

She even had her hair twisted up, with quirky ends creating a crown on top of her head and one long strand framing the left side of her face.

And Alex's fingers itched to set her hair free, to splay his fingers against that flat midriff, to haul her in and torture her into submission.

He clenched his jaw and listened to what she was saying about her progress with sourcing materials, his hands clenched into fists in his pockets.

Merrow had to clear her throat, twice, as she talked Mickey through her part of the weekly update. And it was costing her to keep the calm, businesslike tone in her voice. Especially with Alex standing less than a foot away from her looking so bloody unaffected by her presence.

Apparently *he* didn't even feel the need to so much as look at her, whereas Merrow couldn't stop her gaze from flickering in his direction every damn five minutes.

He had on a suit that managed to make him look half Dublin Alex and half Galway Alex and that was just plain playing dirty! The linen suit was only a shade or two lighter than the hazel of his eyes, and, combined with the white shirt he was wearing loose at the neck, it made his tan look even deeper *and* he somehow managed to look like a man who'd either been recently 'ruffled' or was more than ready to be 'ruffled' any time soon.

It was disgustingly sexy and she hated him for it.

She risked another glance at him from beneath her lashes, her chest cramping painfully, and she faltered on her words again so that she had to clear her throat, *again*. But then, finally, she was done. And she exhaled with relief.

The cavernous room went silent barring the noise of construction in the distance.

Then Mickey D nodded down at the plans, folded his arms across his chest and looked back and forth between them. 'I'm sensing a little tension in the room.'

'The project is going very well,' Alex informed him with a cool gaze.

'And we've started painting on the first floor…' Merrow's words petered off into the silence.

Mickey nodded slowly. 'Mmm-hmm. I got all that. But there's a problem with my team here and I think we should address that.'

Another glance at Alex saw his square jaw clench briefly. It was the first hint she'd had that he was affected by the air between them. But she also knew he'd be spitting nails that their client was witnessing it.

She glanced at Mickey, and saw a brief smile flit across his face before he nodded again. 'I'm thinking we've had a bit of a lover's tiff. I can recognise one of those a mile away. You can do that when you've been married as many times as I have.'

'It has nothing to do with the work we're doing for you.'

And that was probably as close as Alex would allow himself to get to telling a client to butt the hell out.

'Ah-h-h, but a happy team is a productive team, Alex, my friend. Any time we had a bust-up in the band it screwed with our creativity. You gotta talk it out.' He unfolded one arm to wave a hand back and forth. 'Talk to each other. Listen. Even if it's stuff you don't wanna hear. Marquess of Queensberry rules, mind…'

'Mickey—' The warning tone in Alex's voice was all too familiar to Merrow so she stepped in to stop him saying something he'd regret later.

'There's nothing to talk about, Mickey.'

'Oh, I don't think we should *lie* to the client.'

He had *not* just said that! She glared at him with wide eyes. *'Alex—'*

He shrugged his shoulders, his calm gaze focussed on the plans laid out on the reception desk. 'I'm not the one in possession of the rule book here.'

'Except for the rule about what to do or say in front of a client!'

Mickey butted in. 'I doubt there's anything you two could do or say that's gonna shock me. I could tell you tales that would turn your hair grey.'

Alex smiled a small smile and Merrow dearly wanted to strangle him. But the smile disappeared when Mickey continued, 'So what'd you do, Alex? 'Cos in my experience the woman always thinks it's the man's fault.'

'If you can get an answer to that one, then you're a better man than me.'

'Ah-h-h, the old psychic boyfriend radar not working for you, I take it?'

'Not so much.'

Merrow lifted both her arms and let them slap off her sides when she dropped them, 'That's it. I'm done. You two can swap testosterone for the rest of the day; *I* have better things to do.'

'I told you this one was a firecracker.'

'You did, Mickey.'

Merrow pursed her lips together, *hard*, and started shoving her sketches back into her portfolio case. 'I'm leaving now.'

'Well, I'm the paying customer here and I say you're not. Trouble in the team makes for a bad working environment and I won't hold to that. Life's too goddamn short.' Now that he had their undivided attention, Mickey unfolded his arms and walked backwards. 'I'm goin' out front for a smoke and a talk to my manager about the arena tour in the States…'

His hands rose and formed two pointing forefingers. 'And *you two* are gonna stay in here for a half-hour minimum and talk this out. I expect results. All this bad karma might linger in my lovely hotel of seduction…'

He winked before he turned round.

They both stared at the door for a long time after it closed, tension sitting in the air between them like a bad smell.

'I don't believe you just did that in front of him.' Merrow glared at Alex from the corner of her eye. 'What happened to the great Fitzgerald & Son work ethic?'

'Well, it's not like you were in a hurry to come talk to me on your own.'

'Because you made it so very easy for me to do that, didn't you?'

'You knew where to find me.'

'*I'm* not the one that *changed the rules*!'

'Well, maybe it might help if I *knew* the stupid rules!'

It was the first time they'd raised their voices to each other and they both knew it. And the air in the gap between them positively sizzled with anger while they let the fact sink in.

A lone joiner appeared around the corner, took one look at both their faces, and then hastily retreated, whistling in a rising tone that said he sensed trouble.

Alex took a deep breath, took his hands out of his pockets and started to fold his plans up. 'We can't work together like this.'

'I didn't start it.'

'No, Merrow.' He glared at her again. 'The *client* started it! And if *the client* can see when there's something wrong between us, then we're in *real* trouble.'

'You didn't correct him.'

'Because he may be many things, but stupid isn't one of them.' He continued folding. 'And he's right, this needs to be talked about or we're gonna have to find a new way to work for the remainder of this project.'

'You can't fire me.' She lifted her chin, clenching her jaw to stop herself from showing how much arguing with him was hurting her.

'Merrow, I don't want to fire you. You're amazingly talented and you're doing a great job.' He took another deep breath, still folding plans, still not looking at her. 'This has nothing to do with your work; it never has. I've told you that. It's to do with us. And if we can't fix this, then we need to find a way to get through the next few months. Then we never have to set eyes on each other again.'

Which hurt ten times more—and she couldn't speak until she swallowed away the lump in her throat and forced her eyes not to shed a tear.

But even when she *did* speak, there was still a tremor in her voice that she couldn't hide. 'I don't know *how* to fix this.'

His gaze rose and locked with hers, his hands stilling on the paper. 'Do you *want* to fix it?'

'Yes, *I want* to fix it!' She laughed nervously. 'I *hate* this!'

The nod was slow, his gaze intense. 'Me too.'

Merrow stared back at him, unable to move, and unable to go to him when there was still so much between them. 'Honestly? I wish I didn't want to fix it. It would be better if I didn't.'

'Why?'

She avoided his eyes and looked around the room, her foot tapping on the floor the only indication of the inner battle she was waging.

Alex's voice dropped to the deeply seductive tone that always shattered her resolve. 'Talk to me, O'Connell.'

'I don't know where to start.'

'Would it help if I told you what I think?'

She looked at him again, the unreadable expression on his face making her heart ache all the more.

When she didn't say anything he stood a little taller, his broad shoulders rising in a way that looked distinctly defensive to her.

''Cos I've *been* thinking. That's what happens when you won't give me any answers—I go looking for them on my own. So if I tell you what I think, then it might just be easier for you to tell me if I'm right…'

She continued staring at him.

So he quirked his brows and continued. 'I think it's got to do with what I am.'

'An *architect*?'

His mouth quirked; his hands went back into his pockets. 'No, not an architect; a Fitzgerald.'

Merrow almost crumbled. See, he *did* know their families would be a problem. He'd probably known all along—just as she had.

Alex took another deep breath, his gaze still fixed on hers. 'It's *what* I am, not *who* I am. But the problem is the two things are tangled up in each other. I can't change that for you.'

'I wouldn't ask you to.'

'I know you wouldn't. But you can't forget it either, can you?' He frowned and tore his gaze away, taking one hand out of his pocket to shuffle the photographs together on the reception desk. 'I can see how someone like you would find my life stifling. There's a certain responsibility involved with what I am that you might find hard to take.'

Hang on. This wasn't going where she'd expected it to go… But she waited to see what else he had to say.

'The woman that steps into my life won't be run down by the paparazzi or anything like that, but she'll automatically enter into the same responsibilities and duties to the family name that I have. There would be hands to shake and photographs to smile for and a legacy handed down from generations to maintain. That's no easy job. I've always known that—'

A light bulb went off in Merrow's head. 'Because you know it's not easy having been trapped inside it your whole life?'

He flashed a small smile her direction. 'Actually, I'm pretty comfy in my shoes these days. But then I was the one who always knew what was expected of me and fought to live up to it; it was my sister who struggled. Maybe if you ever get to meet her, you'll get to know her well enough for her to tell you about it.'

Merrow thought she'd quite like that. But she didn't say so; she just smiled a small smile back at him. And then another light bulb went off.

'Is that why this place is such a big deal to you? Do you see it as your way of living up to the family name?'

'Ah.' He smiled a self-deprecating smile as he looked around the room, and Merrow felt a small part of her heart giving up the fight. 'Now, you see, you're *almost* right there. I have this goal, you see. You know that plaque outside the office in Merrion Square?'

'The one that says Fitzgerald & Son?'

'That's the one.' He smiled down at the plans. 'Well, I'm kinda determined to have the "& Son" part off there by the end of the year.'

Merrow smiled at the determination in his voice. 'And why is that so important?'

Alex chuckled. 'It's probably going to sound daft to you.'

'Try me.'

He turned round and leaned back against the high desk, folding his arms across his chest before he continued with the familiar hint of a smile on his mouth. 'Each generation of Fitzgeralds adds their own bit to the family history. My father set up the company and made his name as an architect and it's his name that goes first on that plaque.' He shrugged his shoulders. 'And I'm not trying to take away from that or prove that I can live up to it. But I see my part of the bigger picture as opening the company up for the future. If I dump the "& Son" then any child of mine who wanted to take it on wouldn't have to add another "& Son" or an "& Daughter" and if I had a wife who wanted to add to the company in some way then she'd be a part of that plaque too. 'Cos it would be *"Fitzgerald's—"'*

Her eyes warmed when he unfolded his arms to make invisible speech marks in the air in front of his body, his smile growing. 'As in everyone who carries my name. They'd all be part of it. Maybe not one for the annals of history—' another shrug '—but it works for me.'

Merrow didn't think that was daft. Not at all. In fact she thought it sounded just a little bit wonderful. 'And a big success like the Pavenham would be a bargaining point with your father?'

'I said you'd think it was daft.'

'I don't think it's daft.' She dropped her chin, leaning the foot she'd previously tapped onto the heel so that she could twist it back and forth while she looked at him from beneath her long lashes, a coy smile on her face. 'I think I'm a little bit proud of you, as it happens.'

She could have sworn his chest puffed out as he bowed his

head a little, the gold in his eyes glowing. 'Why, thank you, Miss O'Connell.'

Merrow grinned. Lord but he was *something*!

He pushed off the counter, walking towards her in measured steps. 'Now, back to the subject at hand. Before Mickey D comes back to check up on us…'

Merrow stood her ground and waited for him to get to her, her pulse skipping in anticipation.

'I happen to think we had something good going for a while there.'

'I do too.'

'But there's no guarantee with any relationship these days…we both know that. Even without the outside difficulties…'

'Yes.'

'We'd have to just see where it took us. But that would mean dropping the game-playing. No more playboy lover and his mistress.'

'I quite liked the playboy lover part.'

'Okay, that part we can maybe keep. But that then makes you the playboy's lover, not his mistress.'

She began to lift her chin as he got closer. 'I can be that.'

'But I can only help you find your own way with the whole Fitzgerald dynasty thing if you *talk to me* about how you feel.' He stopped a few inches away from her, ducking his head down to search her eyes. 'I don't want you to change, O'Connell, not for anyone and especially not for my family.'

Merrow took the biggest breath her lungs could manage, closed her eyes and let the truth out on a rush. 'It's not just your family we'd have to consider.'

'All right.' He frowned a small frown of confusion when she opened her eyes. 'Now that one I'm gonna need some help with.'

'You haven't met *my* family.'

A flash of amusement crossed his face, 'You told me I was never, *ever* getting to meet your family.'

'And why do you think that might be?'

'Is there some kind of secret hereditary insanity you need to tell me about?'

She grimaced. 'That's debatable.'

'Having spent time with you I might have already had a hint or two.'

She smirked at him. 'You're a funny guy. But, really, you have *no* idea. My parents could crash the entire Fitzgerald family reputation at one sitting.'

'I doubt that somehow.'

Merrow laughed sarcastically. 'Trust me.'

Alex stood tall and pushed his hands back into his pockets. 'Explain.'

'You do know you put your hands in your pockets way too much. It's almost fidgeting. Are Fitzgeralds allowed to fidget?'

'It's to stop me putting my hands on you.'

'I don't remember complaining when you do that.' She smiled a mischievous imp of a smile up at him.

'You see, that look doesn't help. Now stop changing the subject.' He pulled a hand from his pocket long enough to check his wrist-watch before putting it back out of harm's way. 'We have about ten minutes until Mickey gets back. At least five of which I'll need to kiss you in a way I *definitely* can't kiss you in front of a client. So hurry up and explain.'

'My parents are very free-spirited, they never married—'

'If you think for one minute there's never been a Fitzgerald born outside of marriage, then you're wrong.'

'Your family is wrapped in up politics and industry, right? Generations' worth of it?'

'Yep, one Taoiseach, two Tánaistes and one President, though in fairness there were other Fitzgeralds who weren't a part of the family. And we've had at least three heads of state companies.'

Merrow grimaced again, tilting her head from side to side as he reeled it off as if Prime Ministers, Deputy Prime Ministers and Heads Of State were no big deal. 'You see, as far as my lot are concerned, that makes your lot the equivalent of the spawn of Satan. And they'd tell them that, and why, if someone was stupid enough to ask why.'

Alex's mouth twitched. 'I'm taking my hands out of my pockets now…'

'No, Alex—' she dodged back out of his reach '—you need to understand this. Putting your family and my family in the same room would be like standing in the centre of the big red and white target on Easter Island.'

He stood still for a moment, and when she looked up at his face he was wearing a half bemused/half affectionate expression. 'And this is what the problem has been? *This* is what was getting in the way?'

'Dammit!' She stamped her foot in frustration. 'If we try this and it goes anywhere then you automatically merge anarchy into your family! My family would end up in the papers right alongside yours and yours would take the biggest dent to its sense of pride.'

'We've survived the odd scandal before.'

She dodged his hands again, blinking rapidly to clear her vision. 'I can't do it to you, Alex, really I can't. I would never do anything that might hurt you or your reputation. I love my family, with all my heart and soul I do. But I really like you and I can't—'

'Stop it.' He sidestepped her dodge and caught her up in

his arms, hauling her in close to his body and ducking his head down again. 'Stop it, O'Connell. You're getting upset about stuff that hasn't even happened.'

'It *would* happen.' She lifted her hands to his chest, grabbing fistfuls of shirt, because she couldn't *not* touch him, couldn't stop herself from anchoring to his strength. 'I just think we both need to have our eyes open and—'

He lifted a long finger and pressed it firmly against her lips. 'Shut up a minute.'

She frowned at him, and he smiled a slow, deliciously sexy smile before moving his hand to cup her cheek. 'I'm going to kiss you now, if nothing else to get you to stop talking. But first you're going to listen to me. Because we're going to make a new rule.'

'You *hate* rules.'

'No, I hate rules I don't know, there's a difference,' He ran his thumb up and down against her cheek, and watched as her eyes grew heavy. '*No more worrying about this.* You're going to meet my family at the party next weekend, and the weekend after you're going to take me to meet your family.'

'It's my mum's birthday that weekend.'

'Well, then, that's ideal.' The thumb moved to the corner of her mouth. 'And in the meantime, you and I are going to put our families out of our minds and we're going to start over. We're going to *date*; we're going to go out to dinner, spend time with each other's friends, go the movies, go for walks, curl up on the sofa and watch a DVD. But what we're not going to do, much as it kills me to suggest it, is make love to each other. So no sleep-overs for the foreseeable.'

Merrow's eyes widened.

'That plan really sucks.'

Alex chuckled, his warm breath fanning her face, his voice

a husky rumble. 'I know it does, but we skipped all the pre-liminaries before—not that I'm complaining, you under-stand—but maybe what we need is to take a step back in order to catch up. So kissing is still allowed…'

He brushed his mouth across hers to prove the point, and she sighed when he leaned back. 'Touching is fine up to a point…' he brushed his thumb over her bottom lip, touching his fingernail just inside the moist edge '…and PDAs are about to go into overload, just so you know. But that's it. We talk more, about the things we like and enjoy…and I don't mean sex-related things we like and enjoy. I mean stuff that turns on our minds.'

'*You* turn on my mind.'

He smiled that damn hint of a smile and Merrow let her knees give enough to push her body closer into his. 'Now, play nice, O'Connell, 'cos this is going to cost me just as much as it costs you. But if we survive both of our families then all bets are off.'

'I still think this plan sucks.' She stood up on her toes and pressed her mouth to his for a long, slow, deep kiss that left her wanting so much more than she was apparently allowed for the next couple of weeks.

'I know. But humour me.' He groaned when she ran her tongue along his lips. 'Just this one time.'

'I hate you.'

'Right now I hate me too.' Alex turned his head, raising a forefinger. 'Five more minutes, Mickey, old pal. I'm just kissing my *girlfriend*.'

CHAPTER NINE

'YOU'RE Merrow, right?' The stunningly beautiful young woman grinned broadly at her, dimples appearing in both her cheeks. 'I love that name. But not anywhere near as much as I'm *lusting after* that dress!'

She muttered something very fast in fluent French that went clean over Merrow's head.

'I'm sorry—you are?'

She laughed, the sound musical and lilting, and without even knowing an answer Merrow liked her. She was full of life, so very vibrant. And had just enough sparkle in her hazel eyes to let Merrow know they were probably kindred spirits in the mischief department…

'Hell, I'm sorry. I forget sometimes that my infamy isn't known by all and sundry.' She stretched out a long-fingered, fine-boned hand. 'I'm Ashling Fitzgerald, Alex's sister. But you can call me Ash, everybody does.'

'When they're not calling her a pain in the ass.' Alex's friend Gabe, even taller when viewed right side up, tilted his head down to Merrow's ear to mutter the words and then tossed an olive in his mouth, smirking at Ashling on his way past.

Ash waved a hand in dismissal while Merrow shook her other hand. 'Pretend he doesn't exist. I've been doing it for years.'

He took a step backwards to lean in and say something into Ash's ear that brought a faint flush to her creamy complexion and she turned to look up at his face, her eyes narrowing briefly before her lips moved in reply. Gabe's gaze dropped to her lips as she spoke, his broad shoulders shaking as he walked away.

Merrow's brows rose in question, her eyes sparkling knowingly as Ash looked back at her. Because she *knew* that kind of look between two people, didn't she?

'Alex said there was nothing going on with you two.'

Her flush grew but she smiled another dazzling smile, waving her hand again. 'The lump? No. I've known him since I was in nappies, and he's spent half his life with a really bad case of pants-worn-outside-trousers syndrome when it comes to rescuing me from situations *he* deemed to be inappropriate.'

Merrow nodded, her tongue firmly stuck in her cheek. 'Mmm-hmm. I *see*.'

And she really did. In fact, it was reassuring to know she might not be the only woman in the world with the kind of attraction to a man that went beyond common sense. It bonded her to Ash in a way.

Ash turned her face to one side, her eyes narrowing briefly, and she then smiled. 'Oh, I think you and I are going to get along just grand! It's about time I had a partner in crime.'

Gabe came back with a plate groaning under the weight of food. 'She recruiting you to her campaign of terror, then, Merrow? I hope you have a good solicitor.'

Ash nudged him hard enough in the stomach to make him lose an hors d'oeuvre to the floor. 'The only solicitor I'll need these days will be to get a Restraining Order to keep you away from me.'

'Ah-h-h, and the battle begins all over again.' Alex slipped an arm around Merrow's waist, planting a PDA kiss on her forehead before he attempted to steal food off Gabe's plate. 'You wouldn't think they hadn't seen each other in eight years, would you?'

Gabe held the plate out of his reach. 'Get your own, squirt. The buffet's that way.'

Merrow smiled as she watched the warm interaction between the three of them. It was easy to tell they were a tight-knit unit. And even if she didn't have a right to feel like a part of that unit, it made her believe—if just for a moment—that she wasn't really all that different from them. Though she was *very glad* she had on heels again, even if her feet were starting to hurt a little. Without them, surrounded by the three giant beautiful people, she'd have felt like a midget.

But so far, so good, and if the rest of the party-goers were this much fun then Merrow really wasn't going to have a problem with the world of the Fitzgeralds. It all seemed perfectly ordinary to her.

Well, if you removed the largest estate she'd ever been on outside of a National Trust property, and a seventeenth-century mansion that could probably have housed half the population of the island they lived on, that was.

While Gabe and Ash launched into a thrust and parry of words, Alex focussed his gaze on Merrow, a smile lifting his mouth at the sight of the similar smile on her lips. He tightened his arm around her waist and lowered his head to her ear to whisper, 'Surviving, O'Connell?'

She turned her face to his and smiled a very different smile, the kind that once again tested his resolve on his fantastically stupid plan not to make love to her for two weeks. Well, eight days and roughly two and a half hours—not that he was counting. Much.

'So far. Though I'm planning on forcing your sister to tell me *every* embarrassing story from your childhood, just so you know.' She laughed when he slapped a palm against his chest, mock outrage written on his face.

'*My* childhood? Good luck with that. I was the model child, I'll have you know.'

Ash stopped sparring with Gabe long enough to interject, 'Disgustingly, I'm afraid that's true.'

'You balanced him out.'

She ignored Gabe's droll comment. 'But I can show you lots of embarrassing pictures if that helps?'

Merrow's face lit up with wicked glee. 'I'd love that. Lead the way.'

Reluctantly Alex allowed his sister to link arms with Merrow, stealing her away from his side. But he was smiling as he watched them walking away, their heads close together as they talked. If they could be friends that would help, and with Ash back in the country and Merrow enjoying herself at the party, the world felt, well, pretty fine, actually.

It gave him a brief moment of what felt distinctly like hope. He even allowed himself to wonder how she'd react if he told her the thoughts he'd been having of late regarding something resembling the word 'future'?

Frowning down at his feet as he mulled that one over, he absent-mindedly turned over a piece of food on the floor with the shining toe of his shoe.

There was a deep sigh from his side.

'You'll grind that into the carpet, you moron.' Gabe bent over and scooped it off the floor into his hand.

'And you'll make someone a lovely wife some day, you big girl.'

'Hey, once a housekeeper's son, rich boy...'

Alex ignored the comment. 'Where did you say the food was?' He nodded at Gabe's plate. 'If there's any left, that is…'

'We'll have to get together in Dublin some time.'

Merrow smiled as Ash guided her through the crowd and into the long hallway with the huge staircase that seemed to wind upwards and outwards for ever.

'I'd like that.'

It was the truth. She had a suspicion that Alex's sister would fit in very nicely as a fifth musketeer. But then, if things went pear shaped—which realistically they still could—even *that* relationship would add to the fallout, wouldn't it?

She couldn't keep allowing herself to get sucked in by all the 'perfectness', could she? Just because so many things seemed to 'fit' didn't mean she should pretend there weren't just as many things that didn't.

But the thought that she now had to hold back from a potential new friend made her feel, well, sad, she supposed. And the chance of losing Alex from her life had already created a gaping emptiness in her chest of late. Neither one a feeling Merrow much cared for.

'You can take me to where you got that dress. It's vintage, isn't it?'

Merrow nodded, looking down at the dusty rose organdy that crossed the bottom of her heart-shaped bodice and splayed out into a panel that fell over one side of her wide skirt, the subtle painted floral accent studded with sequins shimmering in the light. It had *so* been 'the one' and, judging by how Alex's eyes had glowed when he'd first seen her in it, it had been worth every single extortionate cent.

Wearing it she actually felt that she wasn't all that out of place amongst the elite…

'Nineteen fifties.'

'Well, it's sensational and you look beautiful in it,' Ash enthused, and then turned to point out one of the pictures in front of them. 'This is baby Alex.'

Merrow laughed. 'Oh, now that *is* embarrassing!'

Ash laughed. 'Isn't it? He was a ridiculously cherubic baby. All the more casual pictures are on this wall; the formal shots are in the library. We call this the Family Gallery.'

Hmm. A bit of a different set-up from the hodge-podge of eclectic picture frames Merrow's family had littering every available space on walls and shelves in their cabin... They'd never had a formal shot taken in their lives. And the 'family gallery' had some pretty bohemian shots for the uninitiated...

She glanced briefly at Ash as she released her arm and looked at the pictures. Feeling as if she were being scrutinised from time to time, Merrow wandered along the wall, seeking out Alex's face in each picture. But surely that had to be paranoia? It was more an indication of how a part of her felt as if she were invading a magical world she could only briefly visit—because she'd always be an outsider, wouldn't she?

She saw baby Alex became toddler Alex, toddler Alex joined by baby Ash, every picture showing a happy, normal family just occasionally framed by the backdrop of mansion house to hint they were that little bit different...

Another glance at Ash as she took a sideways step re-affirmed her feeling of being scrutinised. But Ash simply smiled as she reached a hand out to point at a picture in the centre. 'He's six in this one.'

The more pictures she looked at, the more perfect the world of Alex's family seemed to her. They all looked so happy and in every shot Alex was confident, smiling—the golden-boy heir to the Fitzgerald crown...

'That one was taken when he was twenty—the first year he ran the Dublin Marathon. You'll know he set up a charity of his own for leukaemia kids and still runs the marathon for it practically every year. He was one hell of an act for me to follow, *the brat*...'

'No, I didn't know that.' Merrow stared at another picture of Alex with an ancient camera slung around his neck. He was maybe fourteen or fifteen, with a gangly Gabe on one side of him and a grinning pigtailed Ash on the other, their arms over each other's shoulders. Like three little musketeers.

'Mmm.' Ash moved in close to her side and linked her arm again. 'That would be Alex. You know what they say about still waters. Well, he was always the perfect son and never made a big deal out of it—regardless of the responsibilities that came with it. Everything seems to come so easy to him— like he never considers anything he does as being anything out of the norm. But it is. I know that better than most. But then I'm not the perfect one in the family. Like the lump said—I balance him out.'

And there was that word *perfect* again. Surely there had to be *something* dark and horrible in his past—some indiscretion or at the very least a broken heart?

It would help. Because for Merrow, *too perfect* held way more pitfalls than *flawed*. Flawed she understood. Flawed and her were old friends. Yup—the countries of flawed and chaotic bordering on the land of the ridiculous were all places she visited regularly...

But the prospect of a brief visit to the land of perfect was tempting. Especially if it meant she got to be there with Alex. Her stupid heart was already committed to the idea of a holiday—if her head just wouldn't keep thinking she'd be giving up her passport at the border...

Ash ducked her head round and looked up into Merrow's eyes. 'Come on. Let's go pull faces at Alex from the back of the room while he makes his big speech. I haven't got to do that in *years*!'

'Maybe we should get Gabe to help?' Merrow managed a small mischievous smile as they walked back.

Ash lifted her nose in the air. 'Unlike you and me, he has no idea of the meaning of the word "fun."'

'I've got a feeling you could help him with that.'

'Stop it. You're nearly as much of a troublemaker as I am. I think I love you already for that.'

Yuh-huh. The land of perfect even provided a potential sister, *dammit*!

'So what's the verdict, O'Connell?'

'I have to decide whether or not I like your entire family after one night, do I?'

'Oh, yeah, that's right.' He tangled his fingers with hers and swung her arm as he walked her through the darkened end of the house. 'You like to take an average score, don't you? I never did get my mark out of ten.'

She tilted her head and smiled up at him when he looked at her from the corner of his eye. 'It's been so long now that I kinda forget…'

Alex smiled his hint of a smile. 'All right, so that wasn't the best plan I ever came up with. I'm big enough to admit that. But I can't cave *now*, can I?'

'Remind me why you can't?'

He chuckled, the deep sound echoing along the hall. 'Because then you'd have won by making me break my resolve. And I couldn't live with the gloating that would bring my way.'

'Me? Gloat? As if.'

She lifted her nose in the air and Alex chuckled again at her side, his fingers tightening around hers.

'Ash taught you that nose-in-the-air thing, didn't she? It's her trademark move.'

Merrow felt the effects of too many glasses of champagne bubbling up inside her chest, her burst of laughter echoing louder than Alex's chuckle had as she swung on his hand and grinned up at him. 'She's wonderful. I'm glad I got to meet her.'

'So am I.'

Merrow spun on her heel so that she was walking backwards, the affection in his voice and the softness in his eyes an open invitation for her to ask about the relationship that obviously meant so much to him. 'You've missed her, haven't you?'

His brows quirked, as if he was somehow surprised by the question. 'It was just the three of us for a long time; I guess it's felt wrong without her.'

'Three musketeers.'

Alex smiled at her choice of words. 'Everyone should have their own set of musketeers.'

Merrow agreed and loved that he understood it as well as she did. It was something else they had in common, wasn't it? And she knew she was grasping at those connections now.

Taking his other hand, she tangled her fingers, swinging both arms as she continued walking backwards, 'They're there when you need them, are musketeers.'

'They are indeed.'

'You can talk to them about all sorts of stuff.'

'Like how their boyfriends score out of ten…'

Merrow quite liked that he called himself that now; she hadn't even protested when she'd been introduced as his girlfriend all night long. 'They're there with you through the tough times…'

Alex pursed his lips, nodding as he looked over her head. 'Indeed they are.' He took a breath. 'All right, I'll bite—what exactly did that sister of mine tell you?'

When he glanced down at her, she tilted her head and smiled a softer smile. 'What could she possibly have to tell me? Unless you have a deep dark secret you want to share? You know—something to take the "perfect" edge off you... oh, golden child...'

She mentally crossed her fingers.

'No one's perfect.' He lifted their hands a little out to the sides, opening his fingers wide, then wrapping them round hers again. 'Luck. That's all it is.'

'Mmm. *Luck.*' She briefly felt let down that he couldn't have admitted to a flaw; even one. But, oh, no, he had to go and play down the hard work he added to the 'luck' to make his life what it was—which just made him a nice guy on top of everything else. Again. *Dammit!*

All right then. She'd just have to play to the one weakness she knew he *did* have. That way he'd have broken his word. And that was less than perfect, wasn't it?

A stretch maybe—but a start nevertheless.

So she leaned in, pressing her breasts against his chest as she tilted her head and aimed the kind of mischievous imp of a smile up at him that she knew got to him nine times out of ten.

Alex shook his head. 'Uh-uh. I'm not caving in before you, O'Connell.'

'Even if I decide to *make you* cave?'

'It wouldn't *be me* breaking the rules this time, then, would it?' He leaned his head in and focussed his gaze on her mouth. 'Feel free to give it your best shot. But it won't have been *me* that caved.'

'You play dirty, *Alexander.*'

'And you *know* just *how dirty* I can play, *Merrow*.'

Merrow gave a small moan of frustration, her eyes growing heavy, and Alex squeezed her fingers harder in warning, so she batted her lashes at him. And bit her bottom lip.

Which made him groan softly in response. 'You should come with a warning.'

'Oh, I tried warning you off, several times.'

'I knew what I was doing. I still do.'

The gold in his eyes blazed across at her, and Merrow couldn't look away, her heart beating erratically. He studied her eyes, didn't smile, didn't quirk an eyebrow. He just looked at her with a steady intensity that made the ache in her chest so painful she almost moaned aloud again.

She'd thought he was dangerous already. But while he looked at her that way, she suddenly knew exactly *why*—

She needed an escape route. Just for a minute.

'Not yet, you don't.' She avoided his searching gaze as she stepped back from the heat of his body, her eyes watching one of their joined hands as it lifted again, Alex repeating the outward flex and return of his fingers. 'You will in a week.'

When he got to see her *far-from-perfect* world.

They kept making small steps along the hall, their arms still swinging, until Alex's deep voice rumbled above her head. 'It's not really my family that's the problem in your head, is it?'

She still couldn't look at him. 'I had fun tonight. Everyone was wonderful.'

'And you weren't fazed by any of them, not even my parents—though you could have flirted a little less with my father and that would've been okay with me.'

'He was flirting with *me*. I just flirted back. And it was innocent, you know it was.' She smiled as Alex's fingers flexed again. 'Actually he reminded me a lot of you, which probably helped. He has that same sparkle in his eyes when he makes a joke. Though, in fairness, he's probably funnier than you are…'

'At his age he's had more practice.'

'I'll bet he can be hard work sometimes too, though.'

'Then I suppose that's another thing I'd have in common with him.' When her gaze rose to meet his, he smiled. 'Yes, O'Connell. I too am fully aware of my failings. And just like you I choose not to make them public. It works for me.'

If he'd just make even one of those failings public it might help her sort her head out.

But before she could ask, he lifted both their arms again, repeated the flex of his fingers and then she heard the smile in his deep voice. 'We're here—my favourite room in the whole house.'

Untangling their fingers, he turned her around, placing a large hand on each side of her waist as he guided her forwards. And Merrow smiled in wonder at the long room, with its huge arched windows running all along one side and the light from the outside floodlights casting soft arch-shaped patterns from them onto the floor. It was beautiful. Maybe even a little bit magical. Perfect.

'This is the Long Gallery. There used to be family portraits along the back wall, but the light was fading them so they were moved onto the walls alongside the staircases. And the room became a bit redundant—'

She felt his chest rise against her back as he took a breath before he leaned his chin on her head and his multi-toned deep voice began to share some memories.

'Until I made it mine.'

Merrow relaxed back into him as his hands moved so that his arms circled her—one round her waist, one round her bare shoulders—his thumb moving back and forth against her skin as he continued walking them forwards, beginning to sway them the tiniest little bit from side to side as they went along.

'I got *skittles* one Christmas—from *Santa*, of course—so I set them up in here and I'd play for hours. Sometimes I'd even sneak down here in the middle of the night. And then Gabe played too—and we'd have *contests* and *tournaments*.'

She laughed softly as he somehow managed to make it still sound exciting—as if he'd still play, given the chance, even after so many years. And she was almost able to see the two boys in the shadowy room in front of her, laughing and arguing and concentrating on winning.

'Who was the champ?'

Alex lifted his chin and leaned his head down, placing his cheek against her hair and nudging it out of the way with his nose before he spoke softly into her ear.

'Ah—you see the jury's still out. But eventually we decided skittles was a *girls' game*—probably around about the time Ash wanted to play—so we produced a football to kick up and down on rainy days. We smashed a couple of the window panes—got yelled at a few times—ran away and hid a few times…'

He pressed a kiss to her ear, leaned forwards to place another on the soft, sensitive skin a little lower. 'Happy days.'

Merrow tilted her head, allowing him better access to her neck, her eyes closing as burning waves of sensation swept over her body, her voice soft. 'I'm sure you found a better use for the room after dark as you got older, though…secret trysts…first kisses…'

He kissed her neck again; lower this time, so that the end of his nose pressed into the hollow where her neck met her shoulder, where his voice rumbled against her skin. 'If walls could talk…'

Alex plied soft kisses along her shoulder and her breasts grew heavy within the confines of her fitted bodice. Then the arm around her waist shifted higher, his fingertips brushed beneath her breast, his thumb sliding higher to brush back and forth until her nipple pressed against the material. And his mouth worked its way up her shoulder to her neck, his feet still rocking them forwards and from side to side.

Merrow let her head fall back against his shoulder, her hands lifting to rest on both of his, his name a sigh on her parted lips. *'Alex.'*

'I know.' His lips formed the husky words against her skin. 'I want you too.'

When his large hand moved up to fully cup her breast she moaned, turning in his arms to escape the torture, but winding her arms up around his neck anyway, while he continued to rock them. 'Are you caving, Alexander?'

He chuckled, wrapping both arms around her waist to lift her off the ground. 'Are you?'

She was, but, 'You first.'

'Nope, ladies first.'

'You're just *so* chivalrous.'

'Aren't I?' He swung her from side to side, her skirts swirling around her ankles. 'Just a regular Prince Charming, that's me.'

Pretty bloody close when he put his mind to it, as it happened. And therein lay the problem.

'Yes, but I bet Cinderella never wanted Prince Charming to—' She leaned in close to his ear and whispered a lurid suggestion in his ear.

Which drew another low groan from his lips, a hard punishing kiss and a tightening of his arms around her waist before he began to spin her round and round and round until she was squealing with laughter and breathless. Only then did he stop, smiling a fuller, brighter smile than she had ever seen him wear before.

'One more week—*one*—then this is all over…'

Which was exactly what she was worried about.

CHAPTER TEN

'FITZGERALD?'

Alex saw Merrow glance at him from the corner of her eye as her father repeated his name.

He nodded. 'That's right.'

'Not as in Edward Fitzgerald?'

'Who?' Merrow stepped a step closer to his side.

'My grandfather.' Alex set his hand to the small of her back and flexed his fingers in reassurance. She didn't need to worry about him. He could look after himself.

Her father folded his arms across his chest. 'So you *are* one of *them*.'

'Yes, I am.'

'Hmm.' Her father's green eyes narrowed in suspicion. 'I'm not sure what I think about my girl messing around with one of your lot.'

It wasn't much of an opening, but it was one he could use. 'I could say something about the sins of the fathers I suppose...'

His thick brown eyebrows rose slightly in surprise. Then he narrowed his eyes again. 'So what is it *you* do?'

'I'm an architect.'

'Any good at it?'

Alex felt his mouth twitch and forced himself not to smile in case it gave up too much ground. 'Yes.'

'Not like you need to make money at it.'

'Maybe not, but it's what I choose to do.'

The older man jerked his head towards the large picture windows. 'An architect's salary bought you that car, did it?'

'No—'

'Didn't think so.' He gave Alex a look that suggested he'd just lost ground.

'It belonged to my uncle. And it was a mess when I got it, so I bought it cheap and restored it.'

'You mean you paid someone to restore it.'

'No, did it all myself.'

'Hmm.' He stepped closer to the window. 'It's an Aston Martin?'

Alex smoothed his hand across Merrow's back before he stepped over to stand beside him, folding his arms across his chest in a similar stance. 'The DB5.'

'The Bond car.'

'Well, not *the* Bond car. Even a *Fitzgerald* has to draw the line under that kind of price tag.' He was pushing his luck and he knew it.

But Merrow's father simply nodded, unfolding his arms. 'Well, I'd suppose I better see if you did a good job with it, then, hadn't I?'

As he walked away Alex turned on his heel to smile a small smile of reassurance at Merrow, only to have her mother step forward.

'When's your birthday, Alex?'

Merrow rolled her eyes.

'May twentieth.' He raised his eyebrows as he looked at

Merrow, curious as to what relevance that had in the greater scheme of things.

But if he'd waited five seconds he'd have found out. 'Taurus, then. That's a good combination with a Leo. Merrow's a Leo, you know. You'll be very sexually compatible, I take it? That's a start.'

Merrow raised her arms and dropped them, and Alex, after a moment of silence, pointed at her as he moved towards the door. '*That one* I'm leaving with you. I'm going outside to talk cars.'

Well, it wasn't as if he could be in two places at once was it? And cars seemed like the much better option to him—one step at a time and all that. He could win her mother over later.

A thought occurred to him, so he stepped back and smiled his most charming smile. 'Merrow tells me you're a Tantra Master?'

Her mother's face brightened. 'That I am. Do you practise the art?'

'No. But I'd be interested to learn.'

'Alex—'

He ignored Merrow, fully aware that he'd probably pay for it later. 'Maybe you could just walk me through the basics of it.'

'There's a beginners' class this afternoon. You could both join it.'

'We'll do that, then.' A beginners' class couldn't be that dangerous, could it? Not that he knew. But if it involved a few new ideas he could use when the deadline fell—in one day and six hours—then that would make every second of whatever strange stuff he had to listen to worthwhile, wouldn't it?

'No, we won't, Alex.'

'Why not?'

'Because you have *no idea* what you're getting into.'

Her mother patted him on the arm and winked. 'I've been trying to get her into a class for years; seems a shame to me that she denies herself the experience. Don't let her talk you out of it. You'll both reap the benefits.'

'*Mother*—'

'Didn't you hear? "Reap the benefits…"' He nodded his head firmly at her exasperated face. 'And didn't anyone ever tell you, you should listen to your mother? Look what a great job she did with you.'

'Mummy dearest—if you fall for that line I'll know I'm adopted.'

'You're not adopted; you get your good looks from your mother. I'm not blind.'

Her mother chuckled. 'Yes, I think I'm going to like you just fine, Alex—no matter what your last name is.' She patted his upper arm, 'Just don't try that method on her father.'

'I'm hoping the car might help some there.'

'It's certainly a start.'

'Anything else that might help?'

She looked him over and then smiled again. 'I don't suppose you've ever windsurfed? Old fool just decided to learn this summer—there's a school nearby. Better late than never, he says.'

Alex smiled. 'Now *that* I can use.'

He left the room, jogging towards his car, suddenly feeling more optimistic than he had in the few days preceding their visit. Not that he'd ever have used the word 'nervous' if Merrow had pushed him on why he'd been so tense. Prepared for the worst might have been a better description. Mind you, the fact that Merrow had used every weapon in her vast arsenal to try to get him to cave in and *release his tension* hadn't helped.

A little payback in her mother's class was in order…

Merrow shook her head as she walked to the window. *In-cred-ible.* He was trying to pull the same trick with her parents as he had with her friends, wasn't he? And even more incredibly—so far it looked as if it was working! He had the charm of the devil. Damn him.

So why wasn't she ecstatic about that? She should have been…

'*Well*, I have to say he's *very* sexy, isn't he?'

Her mother joined her side and they looked out at the two men surveying the car, both of them standing with their legs slightly apart and their arms folded across their chests—in a very visibly male stand-off.

'That he is.'

'Doesn't let you get away with much, does he?'

'No, he doesn't.'

'Mmm, it was always going to take a strong-willed male to capture your heart, my darling one, wasn't it?'

Merrow didn't answer that one.

'Wanna tell me why you look so smug?'

Merrow frowned when he leaned in to whisper the question. 'Shh,' she hissed back. 'You're supposed to be deep-breathing.'

He took a deep breath and let it out to prove a point. 'I am. Why are you smiling like that?'

She glanced at her mother at the top of the class to make sure she wasn't watching, then leaned in to whisper back with a quirk of her eyebrows, a slow blink of her lashes and a knowing smile, 'You are *so* gonna cave after this.'

'The hell I am.'

She poked him in the chest with a finger. 'Well, we'll just see, won't we?'

'Uh-uh.' He frowned before he leaned back. 'No touching. Your mother said no touching yet. Don't break the rules.'

He watched as her chin rose, the secretive smile growing on her face. And his eyes narrowed in response. What was she up to? Because he didn't see how deep-breathing to a soundtrack of waves crashing could possibly make him cave in when he only had one day, three hours and a handful of minutes to go.

Her mother's voice sounded, with a softly soothing tone that was obviously supposed to add to the ambience, 'And now, the gentlemen moving from your knees to stretch your legs out in front of you…'

Alex adjusted his position accordingly, stretching his jean-clad legs and wiggling his bare toes in the cool air. This was easy, this stuff.

'And ladies moving onto the gentlemen's laps, knees either side of his hips, gentlemen bending the knees to provide support. Making sure there is as little intimate contact as possible and still not using the hands.'

He frowned a little as Merrow raised the sides of her long handkerchief-hemmed skirt and moved into position, her teeth biting down on her lower lip as she concentrated, her gaze flickering up to his long enough for him to know that her lip-biting was also a tool to stop herself from giggling.

He swallowed. All right. He could do this. He could block from his mind the image of the first time they'd made love in his apartment in pretty much the same position. He could pretend he didn't know that underneath that skirt she probably had underwear made of dental floss.

He moved his head from side to side and rotated his neck to loosen the tight muscles.

And Merrow whispered across at him, 'You're not limbering up for a prize fight, Alex.'

It felt as if he were. But he merely narrowed his eyes in warning. He *was not* going to cave in before her.

'And now continuing with the deep breathing, look deep into your partner's eyes, look into their soul and feel the connection building between you.'

Alex waited for Merrow's long lashes to rise, her luminous green eyes looking straight into his. And he looked back, looked deep, a smile teasing his mouth.

She blinked slowly, light from the large windows on one side of the room sparkling in her eyes, showing him glimpses of all the varying different shades of green.

Alex continued to breathe deeply, the tension sliding out of his neck and shoulders. She had sensational eyes. He'd always thought that. He held the smile from his mouth, but attempted to let it show in his eyes.

Hey, over there, O'Connell.

The corners of her mouth twitched, the green in her eyes softened and Alex could almost hear her reply, *Right back at ya, Alex.*

'And breathing deep…'

Alex realised that part wasn't going so well for him any more. He tried hard to focus his mind on it, but while looking into Merrow's eyes it wasn't so easy. In fact his heart was protesting against the lack of air, thudding harder against his chest.

And something in Merrow's eyes had changed too; the twitch at the corner of her lips was gone.

Alex searched the green, and saw something flit across them.

What is it?

Her head shook the smallest amount, so small that anybody who wasn't as close to her probably wouldn't have seen it. But Alex had.

Nothing, she was telling him.

Alex didn't believe her.

'And now I want you to keep looking into your partner's eyes. I want you to think of three words each to describe how you see them, right this minute. Tell them that you can see who they really are. Take turns. One word each. Relaxed deep breathing continuing…'

Merrow closed her eyes briefly and Alex smiled a small smile when she opened them. Ah, communication of the open and honest kind. This class could just prove useful after all. He was a genius.

He quirked his brows, looked deep into her eyes and said the word on a deep, husky grumble. 'Trouble.'

Merrow laughed silently, and then raised her chin a half-inch, the bridge of her nose crinkling, eyes narrowing play-fully as she answered, 'Stubborn.'

Her mother, who had taken to prowling the room, leaned her head down to whisper loudly, 'Not criticisms. Be nice to each other. Let down your guard.' She stood up and moved her upturned palms along the front of her body, 'And *breathe*.'

Alex pursed his lips to keep from laughing, silently clearing his throat to force it away as Merrow looked at him sideways in recrimination. He hadn't actually thought the words were criticisms himself. They were honest. She *was* trouble: trouble of the best kind.

She looked into his eyes and mouthed, *Behave*.

So he took another deep breath, rolled his neck in prepara-tion and then leaned his face a little closer to examine her eyes. It took five seconds for him to smile, but she'd always had that effect on him, hadn't she?

'Beautiful.'

The same something from before washed over the green,

she took a shuddering breath, then a calmer one, swallowed hard and answered with, 'Amazing.'

Alex felt a wave of warmth wash over his chest, his heart beating erratically as he was distracted from her eyes long enough to watch the oh-so-familiar sight of her damping her lips with the end of her tongue. Then his gaze rose and locked with hers, the word a husky, agonised whisper.

'Caving.'

He hadn't meant her, he'd meant *him*. But she understood without him having to explain, her mouth curving up into the kind of smile that made his blood rush in his ears. 'Me too.'

'That's two words.'

'And now we're going to deepen the trust with each other.' Her mother stood at the top of the class again. 'Ladies, set your hands on your partner's face, then allow the tips of your fingers to explore his throat, then over his shoulders, down along his arms. Feel the energy seep through your fingertips; gentlemen breathing deeply and slowly in an almost meditative state. Keeping eye contact—and *breathe...*'

Merrow curled her fingers into the palms of her hands for a moment before she lifted them to his face, watching as his lips parted when she touched his skin. She felt the slight suggestion of new-grown stubble contrasted with smooth skin, she watched his thick lashes flicker, eyelids growing heavy, the gold in his hazel eyes flare.

The sensations were overwhelming.

How could he make every nerve ending in her body tingle without touching her? How could he speed her breathing up with just that look? And how could he not see how she felt when he looked into her eyes?

He smiled the hint of a smile that had always 'got her'. Damn him. Still waters ran deep—that was what Ash had said. And that smile of his was simply a ripple on the surface. Had he never once in his life been like a duck? Okay, maybe not a duck. A male swan maybe—calm and in control and *perfect* on the surface…but paddling like mad underneath?

Heaven knew she'd done her share of paddling. And that paddling had made every achievement in her life seem all the sweeter. *Because* she'd paddled for it…

She ran her fingertips down the column of his neck, her thumbs feeling when he swallowed hard. She watched his thick lashes brush his tanned skin as he slowly blinked.

Never in her life had she been so completely overwhelmed by a man. As if she could drown in those still waters and never feel the need to come up for air until it was too late.

And that scared her. What if she missed the paddling? What if she got so wrapped up in living in a land of perfect happiness that the first time a wave hit she'd have forgotten how to paddle to survive it?

His eyebrows quirked. *What's wrong?*

Nothing. She smiled a small smile to hide behind.

But *his* small frown said he didn't believe her.

She slid her fingertips in beneath the collar of his white shirt, felt the jump of his pulse at the base of his neck and the rise and fall of his chest as his breathing increased, before she lifted her fingertips from his skin and ran her hands along his broad shoulders.

A whisper of a groan sounded. *I'm caving.*

She tightened her fingers around his upper arms as she slid her hands down. *I want you to.*

Her fingertips felt the dust of hair on his wrists and she grazed her fingernails over the skin there, smiling as his eyes narrowed.

'And now the gentlemen repeat the same touches, ladies breathing deeply…'

She let go. *Your turn.*

Alex smiled dangerously. *My turn.*

Payback was about to be hell—because she'd almost killed him with those touches and that look in her eyes. He'd thought he was a strong, self-contained man. But with her looking at him like that, he wasn't. He was weaker than he'd ever felt before. And he should have hated that feeling. But he didn't.

Could she see she did that to him?

A part of him wanted her to. Maybe then she'd understand. Maybe then she wouldn't look the way she had for a heartbeat a moment ago, because that look had worried him.

She took a deep breath and held it as his hands rose to brush her hair off her shoulders. When they framed her face she exhaled on a soft sigh, leaning her face a little to one side while he saw her fight the need to close her eyes.

That's how it felt when you put your hands on me.

Her gaze flickered back and forth, studying his eyes with the tiniest quirk of her arched brows. *What?*

How could she *not* see what she did to him?

He moved his hands down, slid his fingers back into the thick curtain of her hair, his thumbs on her jaw as he felt the erratic beat of her pulse through his palms.

A sigh escaped her parted lips. *I'm caving in.*

He smiled a meaningful smile as he moved his hands along her shoulders, cheating the rules by splaying his fingers so that his thumbs brushed the soft skin at the very top of her breasts. *I want you to.*

Her breathing increased, her bottom lip trembled, she bit down on it, the dark irises in her green eyes grew bigger…

And Alex almost groaned aloud. Because she was doing exactly what she did when she was close to the edge, when all it would take was one of his long fingers to reach down between their bodies, to seek out her moist heat, to flick the end of his thumb over—

He swallowed hard and couldn't help himself, breaking eye contact to look down at her skirt splayed over his legs. Then he realised what he was doing and looked up in time to see her gaze rising too.

And judging by the widening of her eyes and the accusatory lift of her brows, she'd caught sight of the very visible evidence that she wasn't the only one turned on by what they were doing.

Alex shrugged and chuckled silently. *It's your fault.*

He moved his hands down her upper arms and stretched his thumbs out to brush the soft skin of her outer breasts. He glanced down and watched her nipples peak against the material of her blouse.

Merrow gasped, and shrugged his hands off so suddenly that he blinked in surprise when he realised she was struggling to her feet, her cheeks flushed as the occupants of the room all turned their way.

For her to mumble, 'I'm really sorry.'

She leaned over and grabbed two fistfuls of his shirt, hauling him to his feet with a frown. *'Up!'*

Alex somehow managed to scramble to his feet with her hands still fisted in his shirt, a look of amused apology on his face as he was dragged from the room. 'Sorry about this. Please continue. Don't mind us.'

He managed a glance at the smug expression on Merrow's mother's face as she waved her palms along the front of her body again. 'Breathe deeply and relax…'

Outside the door Merrow kept one hand fisted in his shirt as she dragged him all the way down the hall, mumbling beneath her breath.

Alex caught the words, 'Plan sucked…beginning…but, oh, no…'

He grinned behind her. 'And where are we going?'

Outside the doors she spun round and flung herself against him while Alex laughed. 'What are we doing O'Connell?'

'We're caving in—that's what we're doing.'

Both hands again fisted in his shirt, she stood on tiptoe and kissed him, her lips urgent and demanding. And Alex wasn't about to complain, caving in at the same time was absolutely fine with him—they were both winners then.

But when her fingers uncurled and her hands slid under the bottom of his shirt to splay on the warm skin above his jeans he groaned, deep in his throat.

He was already painfully hard, and if she kept up the pace she was setting they were going to end up putting on one hell of a show for whoever opened the door next, so he wrenched his mouth from hers. His hands cupping her face and holding her back from him as they both struggled for breath.

'We can't do this here. *Where?*'

She scowled in annoyance, turning her head from side to side. Then the scowl disappeared, as suddenly as if an invisible light bulb had appeared above her head. 'Can you manage without shoes?'

At that point he'd have run over broken glass if it meant he'd soon be sheathed inside her body. 'I can if you can.'

'Then come with me.' She took his hand in hers and began to run across the grass towards the woods.

While Alex followed behind her, her choice of words enough to make him wish he knew where they were going so they could get there faster.

CHAPTER ELEVEN

THE cabin was so small it was almost a shed. And the trees and bushes had grown so thick around it over the years that anybody who didn't already know it was there would never have even thought to look for it.

Merrow laughed with relief.

Maybe not as magical or as grand as Alex's favourite room, but it was *her* favourite place; her teenage hideaway. No one would interrupt them out here. And she could cry out loud to her heart's content…

Alex's deep voice sounded behind her as they both hopped their bare feet over twigs and bark in favour of softer green patches of moss.

'What *is* this place?'

She grinned broadly when she looked over her shoulder. 'It's my hideaway.'

The light in his eyes danced. 'Is it now?'

She nodded, tangling her fingers tighter round his as she pulled him forwards. 'Yes, *all mine*. This was my "escape from the madness" place.'

'Did you need to escape?'

Merrow sighed, not wanting to lose the sexual momentum

by delving too much into the lack of 'perfect world' she'd grown up in. 'Sometimes.'

'From your parents?'

'There was only ever me and them so that'd be a yes. You try being a teenager in a house where the dinner conversation is about deepening orgasms and aligning chakras, and you'd want the odd five minutes to hide too. Can't you move any faster, marathon-runner boy?'

He must have heard the irritation in her voice, because he tugged on her hand, stopped dead in his tracks and hauled her back into his arms, widening his feet a little before he informed her in a steady voice, 'After all this waiting we're not having a quick fix here, O'Connell. Let's just get that straight. We're going to take our time and we're going to *explore*...'

Merrow sighed. 'It isn't going to take that much damn exploring, trust me. After that dumb class and—'

He framed one side of her face with his large hand, leaning his head in to kiss her softly, his lips whispering from one side of her mouth to the other, effectively stopping her from complaining and making his point at the same time.

But she smiled against his mouth. 'All right, then, just so long as you're inside me and we finish what we started in there, I'll be happy.'

He raised his head a little, his voice husky. 'You were close, weren't you?'

She tugged him forwards again. '*Very* close.'

'So this would be us going to reap some of those benefits, then?'

'Absolutely it would.'

'Do we thank your mother for that over dinner?'

She laughed as she pushed open the door. 'If you do I'll kill you and leave your body in these woods.'

'Nah, you won't do that; you *need* this body.'

More than he could possibly know. But not just his body; she needed *him*. She'd never in her life been so *needy*. And a part of her genuinely did hate him for that; the part living inside of her right next door to the part that was *terrified* by it.

But she could deal with that later. Right now she just wanted him—she wanted to get lost again.

She let go of his hand to search for the plastic containers that held fleece blankets, throwing one out on the mattress of the narrow cast-iron bed before she turned round to look at Alex.

He was surveying his surroundings, his brows rising in question as he stepped towards her. 'You still use this place?'

'When I visit, yes.' She started to unbutton her blouse. 'Could we talk less now?'

Alex stepped forwards and stilled her hands, his gaze locked on hers. 'I'll do that.'

She reached up instead, and began to unbutton his shirt, her knuckles brushing against his heated skin, her body buzzing with anticipation until she had enough buttons undone to set her lips against his chest.

The chest that rose and fell faster as she swirled her tongue, nipped his flesh, her hands working on the buttons lower down as she laid her mouth over his sternum and felt his heartbeat against her lips. She wanted him so badly it was almost desperation.

How had he done that to her?

When he had the front of her blouse open and his hands on her breasts she moaned against him. Lord, it was *agony* and yet *so-o-o* good at the same time. She was officially a puppet—a slave to sex.

Alex swore softly. 'You make me crazy, you know that, don't you?'

Her mouth blazed a course to the hollow of his neck. 'Hmm-mmm.'

She unbuttoned his jeans, her hands shaking as she heard the rasp of the zipper, her knuckles smoothing along the hard length of his straining erection. She wanted him inside her so badly that she could feel her body weeping with the need.

His thumbs gently teased her nipples into taut peaks that pressed against the lace of her suddenly constrictive bra. But she didn't want gentle or slow, she wanted him to take her, the hot and fast way, so that the ache inside her would be gone.

She set her hands inside the band of his jeans and cotton boxers, pushing them both down. But Alex released her breasts and took her hands off him, tangling his fingers with hers and holding their arms out to the sides the way he had when they'd walked along the corridors in his house.

'Slow down, O'Connell.' His deep voice was thick and husky. 'Look at me.'

She'd already looked at him too much in her mother's stupid class. Moaning in protest, she arched her back so that her stomach was pressed against his; skin to skin, she moved her hips across his, smiling in triumph as he groaned. She didn't want to look up into his eyes, she just wanted him to feel the physical need as desperately as she did.

'*Look at me.*'

Oh, for goodness' sake! What did he want from her? Wasn't the fact that she wanted him so badly enough? Frowning, she raised her long lashes until her green gaze met the fiery gold in his hazel eyes. '*What*, Alex?'

But he didn't answer her; he just looked at her with the hint of a smile on the corner of lips that always did so much damage.

Because there it was again: the intensity in his eyes that stole her breath away and made her feel as if she were drowning. Her heart felt as if it were being held in a vice, she couldn't breathe, she could feel her body begin to shake deep down inside, almost as if she were cold—a startling contrast to the heat that burned her skin outside. And he could do all of that to her with a *single look*.

Alex's lashes flickered briefly; he frowned so small a frown that anyone who didn't know him as well might not have seen it. 'There's that look again.'

'Alex—I don't *want* to talk right now.'

'I know, but you need to slow down a little for me. Really— I'm hanging by a thread here. And if you put your hand around me, there won't even be enough time to put on protection. Let me do all the work this time. Trust me to make it even better than it was before.'

She raised her chin defiantly and played her ace. 'We don't need protection. I have it covered.'

His sharp intake of breath was exhaled with puffed cheeks, his frown more distinct this time. 'Since when?'

'Since about two weeks after I met you again.' She tilted her head and smiled a wicked smile, her voice dropping to a low husky tone as she stretched their arms out further from their sides to allow her to step in and rub her aching breasts against his chest.

'Nothing in the way, Alex—you can't tell me you don't want that. Think how it's going to feel when you're inside me…' she leaned up on tiptoes to whisper in his ear '…when you come inside me…'

He swore softly again—was caving in on a whole new level—and she could see it on his face and in his eyes when she leaned back. So she bit down on her bottom lip as she smiled, convinced now that she'd get the hot and fast that she wanted, the version that would make her forget all the emotions that were churning around inside her.

He groaned long and low and set his forehead to hers, backing them towards the bed. 'And now we *really* need to slow down.'

No—not slow. Please not slow.

When she opened her mouth to protest he silenced her with a heated kiss, his lips moving over hers in masterly sweeps before he leaned in even closer, deepening the kiss and forcing his tongue in to seek hers, while Merrow fought to get her hands free and he simply held them tighter, lifting his head to angle it the other way, kissing her deeper.

She felt her heart shift in her chest. It was a weird sensation, like a miniature heart attack might have felt, and with his mouth torturing hers she couldn't gasp for more air and with her hands held trapped in his she couldn't reach out for him to anchor herself as the floor shifted beneath her feet.

Emotion bubbled up inside her chest—she was dizzy—drowning—*please, Alex*!

When he freed her hands and they both frantically removed clothing until there was nothing in the way, Alex kissing her and kissing her until her blood rushed in her ears, she thought she was actually going to win this one time.

But when he set her on the narrow bed and lay down beside her, he lifted his lips from hers and framed her face with his large hands, brushing the hair back from her cheeks, his thumbs moving tenderly against the corners of her mouth as he looked deep into her eyes.

She tried to pull his head closer.

'No. Look at me.'

He lifted one hand from her face to tenderly cup her breast, his thumb moving back and forth over her nipple before he rolled it between his thumb and forefinger, making her writhe in response.

'Look at me.'

Merrow felt frustration building in her aching chest. He was always pushing her, wasn't he? He could be so *demanding*. Didn't he know by now that she wasn't the kind of woman who could be bossed around?

When she attempted to touch him again, he lifted his hand from her breast and guided her hand upwards, her arm above her head, and he wrapped her fingers around one of the wrought-iron bars of the bed-head.

'You can't look at me, can you?'

She closed her eyes, biting down on her lip as he shifted long enough to lift her other arm and place her hand on another twisted bar.

'Why are you still hiding something from me?'

'*Alex—*' She ground his name out from between her gritted teeth, her legs twisting as his hand drifted down her body and slid into her weeping core, one long finger swirling through the moisture.

He leaned his head in, resting his cheek against hers as he whispered huskily into her ear, 'Have I ever told you how much I love the fact that you're always ready for me?'

She fought down the sob of frustration in her chest.

While he swirled his finger deeper, still whispering words of seduction in her ear. 'Even when you try to hide your thoughts—your body never lies…' His breath tickled against her ear. 'Look at me, O'Connell.'

She kept her eyes tightly closed and moaned loudly from between her gritted teeth as her body exploded in a powerful enough orgasm to leave her shaking even harder than before.

Alex raised his head a little, his breath now fanning her cheek as he swore in low surprise. 'I've barely touched you.'

'I told you how close I was before.' She opened her eyes and frowned up at him. 'Not that you were listening.'

When she loosened the hands that had been gripping tight to the wrought iron above her head he looked up. 'No, leave your hands there. I'm not done.'

She was about to protest when his head moved lower and his mouth closed around her nipple, sucking it deeply into his mouth where he swirled his tongue. And she had no choice but to grip the bars and hold on tighter.

How did he *do* that to her? She twisted her head back and forth and fought off the wave of emotion again—wanting the agony to end and never wanting it to end.

He released her breast, blew a puff of cold air over her nipple so that it strained tighter and she moaned again. Then he kissed down her stomach, one large hand moving beneath her knee to spread her legs wider.

Merrow's head rose swiftly. 'Alex!'

Still kissing her stomach, he looked up at her with gleaming eyes. 'Cinderella's request has been stuck in my head for a whole week.'

'If you do that—'

'I know. That's the general idea.' His hand moved her other knee as he lifted his head briefly, his gaze fixed on hers. 'This body isn't yours anymore—it's mine.'

'Alex, you can't just—*ooh-h-h*—' She'd been going to tell him that he couldn't possess her like some inanimate object, but her reaction to the first touch of his tongue would have made a complete liar of her. As would the sounds she made while he continued to worship her with long sweeping touches interspersed with shorter, sharper flicks. He was *killing her*!

But even while she felt the rolling waves growing in intensity again, her hips straining up and then being held in place by his large hands, she also felt overwhelmed. Lost. As if a part of her had surrendered and she would never, ever get it back.

'*Alex—*' *Stop. No, don't stop. Dear Lord.*

'Mmm-hmm?' The vibration of his reply tossed her right over the edge again and she screamed aloud.

She clamped her eyes shut. It was too much. She couldn't do this. The second she'd decided to launch into an affair with him had been the beginning of the end for her. *No more Merrow*— just O'Connell—*his* O'Connell. That was what it felt like.

She fought the tears, because she wouldn't cry in front of him. She couldn't give him *that* as well!

Alex's voice sounded closer, she could feel the tip of him poised between her legs, his deep voice demanding. 'Look at me, O'Connell.'

'I can't.'

His voice was gentler, she felt his arms shake the bed on either side of her as he supported his weight while he slid oh-so-slowly into her body, stretching her still-trembling muscles.

'Yes, you can.'

'Alex, please—' She could hear the tremor in her voice, and to her ears it sounded as if she was begging. Just as he'd made her beg him before.

He slid out until he'd almost left her, his arms shook again, he slid forwards and she could hear his ragged breathing as he fought for control.

Somewhere in her tangled thoughts she realised that in this one thing, if not in anything else, they were equal. She could bring him to the brink and throw him over the edge just as fast as he could her, couldn't she? To test the theory while she swallowed down the lump of emotion lodged in her throat she contracted her inner muscles and the move drew an almost strangled groan from deep in his chest.

'*O'Connell*—look at me!'

She smiled, determined to find the strength to torture him

in retribution for everything he was making her feel. So she forced the emotion back down into her aching chest again and opened her eyes.

Alex's face was flushed, his eyes sparkling with gold, his lips parted as he took shaky breaths. And he moved his hips again, slid back until he'd almost left her, slid back and groaned when she tightened around him again.

Merrow gripped the bars harder, she bent her knees and pushed her heels into the mattress, and she took shuddering breath after shuddering breath while her body shook on a whole new level.

She shouldn't have opened her eyes. She shouldn't have looked up into his gorgeous face.

Alex frowned down at her. She saw the inner battle in his eyes as his body tensed for release. And then the image blurred as she felt the knot low in her abdomen disintegrating, wave after wave after long, rolling wave of pleasure cascading out and up, to where they washed over her aching heart.

That was when she heard him groan out his release, when she felt the rush of warmth inside her body—and when she was finally aware of the tears streaking down into her hair at either side of her face.

Alex went still, a sudden patter of rain on the tin roof of the cabin filled the silence, and Merrow closed her eyes tight again. Damn him—damn him—*damn him*!

She didn't want to be this much in love.

The softly spoken words tore her apart at the seams. 'What is it? What's wrong?'

She shook her head, releasing her hands so she could push against his chest. 'Leave it alone. Just this one time.'

'I can't, O'Connell.' But he slid from her body anyway, as if he somehow knew that she needed the space.

And she did.

She moved swiftly, squirming off the bed to gather her clothes while she swiped angrily at the dampness on her cheeks.

Alex took a deep breath. 'We need to talk.'

'No, we don't.'

'Yes, we *do*.'

Merrow swore beneath her breath as she dodged his outstretched hand and hauled her clothes on. She'd never had any body issues before, but after the soul-deep connection she'd just felt to Alex she'd never felt so stripped bare before. And she needed the covering as an extra defence while she tried to deal with her emotions.

'I don't want to bloody well talk. I told you I didn't want to talk when we *got here*.'

'Something just happened and I want to know what it was.'

'And we're well aware of the fact that Alexander Fitzgerald always gets exactly what he wants, doesn't he?' She spun on him as she pushed her arms into the sleeves of her blouse, her vision still swimming, which made her even angrier.

Alex frowned darkly at her as he zipped his jeans and fumbled with the button. 'What does *that* mean?'

She tilted her head and practically spat the words at him. 'What do you *think* it means?'

'Would I *ask* if I *knew*?'

She scowled at him. 'Leave it alone. Just this one goddamn time, stop *pushing* me!'

Alex's face fell, and she hated him for the vulnerable husky edge to his deep voice. 'I can't.'

Because that expression coupled with that tone brought a fresh wave of agony into her chest, and her vision swam even more. He looked as if she'd hurt him, and, despite what she was currently doing and saying, she didn't want to hurt him.

She just didn't want to love him *this* much.

So she shook her head and dodged past him as he reached a hand out for his shirt, hauling open the door and running out into the rain.

'Wait! O'Connell—damn it—wait a minute!'

Trying to outrun someone who ran marathons probably wasn't the wisest decision she'd ever made. But she knew the path better than he did, and once she was on the lawn she sprinted, her heart beating so fast that she could barely catch her breath.

But when she yanked open the door and ran straight into her father, Alex was right behind her, skidding to a halt on his bare feet, hopping a couple of times to get his balance, while they both gasped for breath.

Merrow tried to step past her father, but he held her arm, examining her face for a moment before he set her a little behind him and jerked his head to indicate Alex should come in.

She glanced briefly at him standing inside the open door, his shirt buttoned unevenly, his chest heaving, raindrops running down his face from his wet hair. But when he frowned in pained question and swallowed hard, she looked away. It hurt too much looking at him.

'Which one of you wants to tell me what's going on?' Her father examined their faces in turn before he automatically jumped to his daughter's defence with an accusatory pointing finger. 'Did he *do* something?'

Merrow twisted her arm free and crossed her arms over her chest. 'No.'

'Bloody looks like he did.'

'I—' Alex was silenced with a glare.

'I'm speaking to my girl.' He looked back at Merrow. 'So what's going on?'

'Dad—' her voice shook '—he didn't do anything. I just need some space, that's all. I can't think when he's there—I can't—he's just so… He didn't do anything wrong. Please, just leave it alone.'

She saw the slow spark of understanding in her father's eyes and it made her angrier still. 'Why can't you *all* just leave me alone? Why does *everything* have to be talked through? Why just *once* in my life—' She stamped her foot in frustration as she sobbed again. 'Not everyone wants every single little tiny feeling analysed to death and then lined up with the bloody *cosmic forces*!'

When Alex tried to follow her, one arm stretched out and blocked his way. 'Leave her. I've seen this before. If you keep pushing her she'll only fight harder. It's what she does. She's always been that independent that every decision has to be hers and hers alone.'

Alex frowned hard, and then took a deep, shaky breath as he ran his hand over his face. 'I might have needed that information a little earlier.'

His mobile phone rang, breaking the silence. And Alex frowned in apology as he fished it out of his pocket to switch it off.

'Go ahead and take the call.'

'No, it's—'

The older man shrugged. 'Go ahead, Fitzgerald. I've a feeling you and I will have time enough to chat, judging by *that* episode.'

'I hope so.'

He nodded. 'Answer your phone. There's probably some national crisis you need to avert or some striking workers you need to diddle out of a pay rise…'

'Can't say we architects have those problems.'

'*Hmm.*'

* * *

'Finished with your tantrum, my darling one?'

Merrow ignored her mother's bright tone. 'Do you know where Alex is?'

'Oh, I'd say he's putting his things in his car by now. He popped in to apologise for leaving,' She continued setting food out onto plates. 'He brought me the loveliest birthday gift—did you see it?'

'He's leaving?'

'Yes, some problem with his hotel, apparently; I said we'd see you back to Dublin tomorrow so he—' She was talking to an empty room.

Alex saw her coming from the corner of his eye and took a deep breath in preparation.

A couple of feet away she stopped, and folded her arms across her chest. 'Not bothering to say goodbye?'

'I would have if I knew where you were. I said goodbye to your parents.' He threw his bag into the boot of the car, still not able to look at her. Because if he looked at her it was gonna hurt, wasn't it?

'So you just thought up some excuse to leave?'

'No.' He took another deep breath. 'I got a call from Gabe. There was a fire on one of the top floors at the Pavenham and—'

'A *fire*?' She stepped forwards, her arms unfolding, 'How bad a fire? Is there much damage—'

'It's not as bad as it sounds, Gabe said. Someone left one of the large heaters they use to dry out the walls on overnight. And something must have fallen on it. But I still need to see it for myself.'

He could feel her eyes on him as he slammed the boot shut and walked around the car—he even chanced another sideways glance to confirm he was right—and he hated that she lifted her chin and refolded her arms.

'So you're using it as an escape route.'

He pursed his lips hard and glared at her from the corner of his eye. 'I'm not having another argument with you. I'm giving you space.' Another deep breath. 'Maybe it's what you need right now.'

When she didn't say anything he yanked opened the driver's door. Only to be stopped dead by her words.

'Well, you've seen for yourself now anyway. Now you know our family backgrounds are too different, so you—'

The door slammed violently and he swung round. 'All right, *now* we're having an argument.'

She visibly baulked as he approached her, but he didn't care how angry he looked.

'This has nothing to do with your family or mine or whether or not they'd all kill each other over Sunday lunch— so stop hiding behind it! Whatever the hell the problem is is in *your head*. And I can fight for this, Merrow, but I can't fight for it on my own!'

He saw the brief hesitation, saw her eyes glitter, and it almost killed him. But when he automatically reached out to her to try and fix it, she stepped back from him, her voice rising.

'Stop it, Alex! You've been pushing and prodding and crossing every line on God's green earth to win this battle with me and I've had enough! Why couldn't you just leave things the way they were?'

He tilted his head and threw the answer back at her. 'Why do you think?'

'Would I *ask* if I *knew*?' She threw his own words back at him, her arms unfolding so she could point an angry finger towards the ground at his feet. 'This is all some big game for you, isn't it? I may be what you *want*, Alex, but I'm not what you *need*! 'Cos I'll never be the kind of woman that'll fit into this near-perfect blueprint you have for life. How can you not know that by now?'

He laughed incredulously. '*Perfect?* You think my life's *perfect*? Where did you get that from?'

'Of course it's perfect! You're the Fitzgerald golden boy! Even your own sister had problems following behind you. Everything comes so easy to you and you—'

'Easy? Is that what you think? You think I just breeze my way through the day?' He swore. 'You think I don't work damn hard at every single thing I do? You think I haven't worked *for this*? Because let me tell you something, Merrow, I've never worked harder at any relationship with a woman. *Ever!*'

'Only because I'm some kind of challenge to you! You don't need the kind of chaos I'd bring to your life—'cos, trust me, Alex, I *would*. My life is and always has been a *glorious* kind of chaos. And I *love* that!'

'And what would you know about what *I need*?' He threw a hand out to his side. 'You're such an expert on my life, so go ahead and tell me what it is *I need*.'

'You don't need *this*!'

He scowled at her. 'You're damn right I don't need *this*! But then no matter how many times I try to get you to talk to me, you won't tell me what *this is*!'

'And there you go *pushing me again*!'

It took every single ounce of self control he had not to continue yelling back at her. And it took more than a minute for him to get himself under control before he could even look at her again. So he studied the trees behind the house—he looked at the flowers in pots on the window sills—and all the while he pursed his lips, clenched his teeth and fought with his emotions; willing them down into place inside him.

He took a step closer, his gaze fixed on the top of her head, his voice low and threaded full of the emotion he was fighting. 'I'm done pushing. You've had me battling you for every inch of ground since the day I met you and I've had it.'

'So this is us breaking up.'

A quick glance into her shimmering eyes told him that the calm tone to her voice had cost her, so he kept his voice equally calm. 'No, this is me telling you *no more pushing*. I'm giving you the space you want to think this over. And then maybe you'll actually talk to me about whatever is going on in your mind.'

Her voice shook. 'It's not space I want—'

He couldn't stop himself, swearing violently as his arms swung out to his sides again. 'That's just it—you don't know what it is you *do* want—*do you*? And maybe what it really comes down to is that I'm not the one *you* need. Maybe it'll take a stronger man than me, because, no matter how many times I try to stop myself, I just keep on crossing the line with you, don't I? And the thing is—I can't tell you I'll ever stop doing that!'

'*Why*, Alex? Why can't we just be the way we were when we laughed and played around and had amazing sex?'

He leaned in until his face was right above hers. 'When you figure that out maybe you'll come find me. And if you don't then I'll know where I stand, won't I?'

He turned on his heel and marched back to the car, his hand on the door handle while he attempted to force his heart rate down to one that didn't feel as if he were one step away from a coronary.

Then he spun round and marched back to her, grabbing hold of her so suddenly that she rocked back on her heels. And he wrapped his arms around her, bent her backwards and kissed her, putting every ounce of frustration and anger and passion and wanting and need into the kiss as it was physically possible to do, before he set her back on her feet and released her.

'That's in case you *don't* come find me.'

Merrow stood in one spot and watched him walk away, watched him get into his car and watched him drive away without looking back. Even when it started to rain again she stood there, with her arms wrapped around her body to try and stop the shaking, and with tears running freely down her cheeks. She finally let the first sob out, looking towards the sky as rain poured down on her upturned face.

And she didn't know how long she stood there before a voice sounded beside her. 'I've brought you some chamomile tea.'

She laughed through her tears as she looked at her mother. 'That's not gonna do it this time.'

'You're dreadfully in love with him, aren't you?'

'Yes.' She sniffed and set her palms to her face to scrub away her tears. *'Dreadfully.'*

'And do you know how *he* feels?'

'Sometimes I think I do—' she swallowed '—but he seems to have just as much trouble communicating with me as I do with him when it comes to actual emotions.'

Hang on. That was a flaw, wasn't it? It made him less than perfect—it made him as human as she was. Because maybe, just maybe, when someone cared deeply, it meant they guarded all the more against being hurt? And if he loved her anywhere near as much as she loved him—

What had she just done? Had she missed all the signs? What *hadn't* she seen that'd been there all along?

'Hmm.' Her mother linked their arms and turned them around. 'Did you *see* my birthday present from him?'

CHAPTER TWELVE

ALEX trudged his way up the stairs to his apartment, feeling wearier than he had in his entire life. He'd blown it with her, hadn't he? He'd pushed too hard.

But even while he'd decided he couldn't do anything more, he'd still gone out and tried to find another way to let her see how he felt. He was officially pathetic.

He lifted the plastic bag out in front of him as he climbed the last few stairs. 'I don't know what I'm gonna do with *you*.'

Fitting his key into the door, he took care not to swing the bag as he walked through, and then, when he looked into the kitchen, the first thing he saw was the bowl on the end of the counter.

He frowned in confusion as he stepped forwards, glancing around the empty room before he leaned down to look through the glass, his heart rate picking up speed.

'I take it you're Fred? Did I know you had a key to my apartment? Wasn't it a bit hard to fit into the lock with fins for hands? That's quite a trick, Freddie boy…'

'You gave *me* a key so I could get in for brunch.'

He stood upright and watched as Merrow walked along the hall towards him, a small, almost shy smile on her face—which was endearing as all hell, because he'd never once pictured her as *shy* before.

'Hi.' It was all he could manage.

'Are you two bonding?'

She kept walking towards him, her voice low, and maybe even a little nervous? Well, if that was what it was then she wasn't alone. He was torn the way he always was: between reaching for her or pushing her for answers. But then she'd had him suffering the sweetest kind of misery that way for a long time, hadn't she?

He silently cleared his throat, his gaze catching sight of the folded sweater in her hands. Had she come by to collect anything she'd left behind? Well, if that was the case, then why had she brought Fred along?

'So you were just taking Fred for a walk and you decided to come get your stuff?'

He set the plastic bag on the counter beside Fred's bowl and watched her gaze shift to study it.

'Did that bag just move? What's in there?'

He folded his arms. 'My question first.'

She quirked her eyebrows at him, held one foot out to her side, and pointed. 'You think I went walking my goldfish in *these heels*?'

Alex felt a bubble of hope form in his chest. 'Please tell me you don't actually take your goldfish for walks.'

Her smile grew. 'What's in the bag?'

All right then—this had been *his* bright idea anyway. One more risk at humiliation and then that was *it*. So he lifted the bag in one hand and reached into it with the other, holding the smaller bag up in the air by his face as he pointed at it.

'*This* is The Wilma Two.'

'Alex—' she walked towards him again, tilting her head to one side as she smiled the mischievous smile he loved so much '—you can't name a goldfish the way you name a boat.'

'The way I see it, he who buys the goldfish gets to name the goldfish.'

She stopped a foot away from him. 'And is Wilma—'

'*The* Wilma—' he nodded '—Two.'

'*O-kay*. Is *The* Wilma Two here to keep *Fred* company?' *Okay, Alex—there's your opening.*

'*Her* life may be perfectly fine in this wee bag, but it's not what it *could* be. And even an independent, free-spirited goldfish should know *she* doesn't always have to be alone to still remain independent and free-spirited.'

Her green eyes shone brightly as she bit down on her bottom lip to keep control of her smile. But when she turned and set the sweater down on the counter opposite him, he saw her hands shake and his heart jolted in his chest. Had he just pushed too hard again?

She turned to look at him, swallowing hard and taking a deep breath before she spoke. 'All right. I'm going to go first. But you have to promise me you'll not say or do anything to interrupt me until I'm done, okay? I've been rehearsing this all the way back from Dingle and if I don't get it all out in one go then I might mess it up.'

The bubble of hope in his chest fizzled away, like the air being let out of a balloon. But he merely took a similar deep breath and leaned back against the opposite counter, pushing his hands deep into his pockets.

'Okay.'

Merrow's eyes followed the movement and she smiled a small soft smile. Because she knew what it meant when he put his hands in his pockets, didn't she?

Her gaze flickered up to meet his, she took another breath, and then she set her hands on the counter and hoisted herself up onto the surface, locking her heels at the ankles.

When she set her hands on the short skirt of her green dress Alex watched them shake again; he watched her flex her fingers in and out of her palms and a sense of impending doom rolled over him.

'Look at me, Alex.'

His gaze rose. And she smiled tremulously, staring at him for a long moment before she glanced upwards and then back into his eyes.

'I am so incredibly, completely, to the very pit of my soul in love with you, Alex. And that scares me to death—really it does.'

He'd never wanted to reach out for her so badly before, had never had to fight so hard not to speak. Especially when her lower lip trembled, her hands shook again, and when every word she said was highlighted by the quirk of her arched brows or the flicker of her long lashes so he knew how much she meant the words.

She loved him?

She smiled at the expression on his face. 'Let me get it all out.'

Alex swallowed hard and nodded. If she had a 'but' in that speech anywhere he may just forget it. She was his now and that was that as far as he was concerned; he didn't give a damn how much she yelled at him or tried fighting him. She was *his*.

'I've been independent my whole adult life. And I love my life, Alex, I do—chaos and all. I have great friends, support from my family—albeit of the "being at peace with my inner self through meditation" kind of support—and I have a job I love doing. I pay my own way, I *love* to shop, I can go away on weekends to places like Galway at the drop of a hat.' She took a deep breath and glanced away and back again. 'I never thought I needed anything else, not really, *until you*.'

'I don't want to take any of those things away from you. I thought you understood that. I never have.'

She frowned briefly and then sighed. 'I do know, Alex—I *do*—but loving you is such a big, all-consuming thing it knocked my perspective off, is all. I had *no idea* love felt like this. When you look into my eyes all intense the way you do, I get *lost*. And when you make love to me I don't know where I end and you begin.'

He smiled softly at her.

And she smiled softly back. 'It was like I was giving up a part of myself by wanting you the way I do. It felt *too* perfect, *too* right and that scared me to death—because I thought if I had something that perfect and that right, even for a little while, then losing it would finish me—at least for a decade or two. I just don't think I was ready for it to happen so fast. And when I got scared, I got defensive, and I tried to run from it; to give it rules and boundaries to keep me out of harm's way. But I don't want to run. I just don't want to feel this lost any more.'

Well, that's it all out in the open now—you've taken your shot...

And it wasn't actually as hard as she'd thought it would be, now that it was done. She'd just needed a little shove in the right direction, hadn't she? A validation of sorts. And the present he'd given her mother had done the trick...

'You done now?'

'Almost.' She damped her lips and took another breath, because this was where she had to take the real chance. And if she was wrong then she might as well find a tall building to jump off. 'Now we move on to you.'

He looked suspicious. 'What about me?'

'Well, I think maybe I always knew it was me that was going to have to say the words first. Because, to be honest, if you'd said them I'd have felt backed into a corner—would probably have argued with you and run again.' When he frowned she smiled at him to let him know it was all right. 'I'd have come back eventually, don't get me wrong. But if you'd said it before I knew how I felt—I'd have felt—I don't know…'

When she searched the air above her for the right word, he filled it in. '*Beholden* to say it back?'

She smiled all the more. 'That's a deliciously old-fashioned word. But, yes, I suppose its close. Not *completely* right, though. I was determined I could stop myself from falling for you, you see.'

'Hence all the stupid rules.'

'Yes—but then you would just keep on breaking them…so this is all your fault really…'

'And why do you think I did that?'

He was still leaning against the counter, he still had his hands lodged firmly in his pockets, but one glance was all it took to see the intensity in his gaze and even from a few feet away she could see the gold flecks blazing at her.

And she felt the same something pass between them that had the day they'd taken her mother's silly class. Maybe there was something to all that after all; she'd certainly been right about the *reaping the benefits* part…almost a little *too* right. Because it was all about deepening soul connections for a deeper sexual connection, wasn't it? Or something. Merrow just hadn't been prepared for how it felt, was all.

But then maybe it'd just been the fact that it was the first time he'd made love to her when she'd faced how she really felt? And the depth of that emotion had made the experience so overwhelming for her that she'd folded. And run. Literally.

Maybe if she'd known he felt the same way…

Suddenly feeling more confident with the evidence she'd brought along, she smiled a small mischievous smile and swung her legs.

'Ah, now, you see I wasn't *entirely* sure about why you were doing it.' She rolled her eyes. 'Blind idiot that I am.'

He smiled his hint of a smile and a sense of joy consumed her.

'Until I got to see *that*.' She jerked her head to her right and watched as his gaze moved.

He looked at her from the corner of his eye. 'You *stole* your mother's birthday present?'

'*Borrowed.* You do know I did Art Appreciation in college? We're taught to read meaning into things like that. It's my evidence.'

He pursed his lips and nodded, then turned his head to look into her eyes again, nodding in her direction. 'So am I allowed over there yet?'

'Frankly I'm amazed you've stayed put for as long as you have. I must be losing my touch.' And it might even have helped with her sense of vulnerability as she told him how she felt if he'd been closer. But then she *had* told him to stay put…

Yup. *Still* her own worst enemy.

He chuckled as he took his hands out of his pockets and stepped forwards. 'Oh, you're not losing your touch, O'Connell. Staying over here has taken every ounce of self-control I have.'

'You see, I remember a time when I used to be able to make you *lose* your self-control…'

'More than any other woman ever has.' He slid his hands up the outside of her legs and underneath her crumpled skirt, until they rested on her hips, his deep voice laced with tenderness. 'Or ever will.'

She bent to the side and picked up the framed photograph, holding it in front of her body. 'So tell me about *this*. Did you do Art Appreciation at any point?'

Alex nodded firmly, his fingertips moving against her skin. 'I did.'

'We-ell, then you knew what you were doing with this, didn't you, *Alexander*?'

He smiled ruefully, his gaze locked on hers. 'I'm never going to hear the end of this, am I? Years from now you're still going to drag it up—and when we go to visit your parents you're going to look at it and smile smugly, aren't you?'

She nodded as firmly as he had. 'Yes, I most certainly am.'

She unlocked her ankles, opened her legs, wiggling her backside forwards on the counter so that he could step closer, and then she held the photo up in front of his face. 'So what does this photograph tell us?'

With a sigh he peeked over the edge. 'Why don't you just tell me what you see?'

'Okay, then, I will.' She grinned as she turned the photograph round, holding it pressed against his chest while she forced the grin away and mock-frowned with concentration, her voice in 'Art Appreciation' mode. 'The central focus of this photograph is a girl in a green dress—that being *me*, you understand—in the dress I'm currently wearing, as it happens, not that you've noticed…'

'O'Connell, I only ever see *you*.'

'You see when I have a short skirt on.'

'All right, that I *do* see.'

'Shh.' She frowned at him again. 'I'm not done.'

Alex rolled his eyes.

And Merrow laughed before she put her concentrating face back on. 'The girl in the green dress is in colour, she's *in focus*, whereas the background is in shades of grey and *out of focus*— it's all blurry.' She tilted her head and quirked a brow at him, batting her long lashes. 'So what does *that* tell us?'

Alex shook his head, his mouth twitching. 'You're gonna pay for this, you know.'

'*What* does it *tell us*, Alex?'

'You tell me. I just took the damn photos.'

'And then put the shots together so beautifully.' She planted a swift kiss on his mouth. 'So if I was interpreting this photo I would say that it looks like the girl in the picture—i.e.: *me*—is all that the photographer—that's *you*—sees. Everything else goes blurry around her when he looks at her; she's maybe even—dare I say it?—the *centre of his world*?'

Alex removed a hand from under her skirt to snatch the photograph from her hands and set it, face down, on the counter. 'All right—*enough.*'

He removed his other hand too, both of them framing her face, fingers sliding into her hair, thumbs stroking her cheeks, and then he leaned his head in closer to hers, his voice husky.

'You got me. You had me on the bridge that day, O'Connell. O'Connell on the O'Connell Street bridge, ironically enough. But you got me—I couldn't see anything else. I think I fell in love with you that day.' He smiled. 'Not that I'd have admitted it to myself at the time.'

Merrow reached her hands forwards, wrapping her arms around his lean waist to tug him closer. 'Keep going.'

Alex blinked slowly, his eyes full of emotion she could finally *see*, almost as if the deep water that had been too cloudy to see through had suddenly taken on a Mediterranean-sea clearness, so that she could see all the way to the bottom and all the wondrous sights that had been hidden from her.

'It's not *all* my fault, you know. You helped. An affair wasn't enough for me, O'Connell; it wasn't anywhere near enough. So I started to break the rules one at a time—I figured if I did it that way rather than telling you I wanted more, then

I might get you to realise that what we have is way too deep to ever be just an itch to scratch…'

Merrow sighed contentedly, leaning in to place another, softer kiss on his mouth. 'Keep going.'

'You want every single part in one go?'

'Yup.'

He bent in for another soft kiss. 'I tried to show you we could work by charming your friends—'

'At disgustingly record-breaking speed. But then the musketeers were always suckers for a pretty face…'

'Do you want all of this or not?'

'I'll behave,' She bestowed another kiss on his mouth, then leaned back and waggled her eyebrows ridiculously. 'And I promise to reward you for every single detail…'

'I'll be quick, then.' Another kiss. 'I tried to show you how I felt when I made love to you, but you still weren't getting it, so I "coaxed you" into sleepovers so I could hold you in my arms all night and you'd see that we'd be able to live our everyday lives and still make time for each other. I reckoned asking you to move in would have been pushing my luck—'

'It would have.'

'See, I knew that. So then I went away for a weekend to try and give you the opportunity to miss me—'

'You said you had that booked for months!'

'I was a last-minute sub—' he flinched when she kicked the back of his leg '—but it *backfired*. Because I just ended up missing you so much that I pushed my luck again on the phone by telling you you'd nothing to worry about. And you don't. You're *it* for me—chaos and all. No matter what you may think, my life isn't anywhere near perfect unless you're in it.'

She smiled at the choice of words. 'And you're *it* for me. I'd rather feel lost *with* you than *without* you.'

He grinned and rewarded her with another, longer kiss. 'You're not lost, O'Connell. You don't ever need to feel lost again, 'cos whatever you give of yourself to me you'll get back a hundred times over. I promise.'

'I love you *so* much.' She grinned back at him. 'You done confessing all the things I was too blind to see?'

He moved his hands from her face to wrap them around her waist. 'I could say yes and just go ahead and get my *reward...*'

'You see, that won't work 'cos I now know there *is* more. So hurry up. You'd just done the part where karma got you for fibbing to your girlfriend...'

'Well, then, of course, I conned my way into your apartment so I could try and wriggle my way into your life a little further. But that didn't go so well...'

'That was me starting to fight how I was feeling.'

'I know that *now*. But I didn't let it go, did I? So then we moved on to the part where I tried to prove to you that our families didn't have to get in the way. Though of course I now know that that wasn't really the problem. So long as we're this strong, O'Connell, nothing they do will get between us—*ever.*'

'I know.' She leaned in for another kiss. 'But there'll be cringe-worthy moments every time they're together—be prepared.'

'Stuff them.' Another kiss. 'We'll lock them in a room and let them fight it out. Now where was I? Oh, yes...you fitted in beautifully in Fitzgerald land—'

Merrow moved her arms from around his waist and began unbuttoning his shirt. 'I quite liked Fitzgerald land.'

'You'll make an amazing Fitzgerald.'

'Is that a proposal, Alex?'

'I thought you'd have guessed you'd get one of those some

day when I talked to you about my wife adding to the business and knowing her name was on the plaque.'

Merrow tilted her head, her fingers still working on buttons as she smiled impishly at him. 'I did think that sounded just a little bit wonderful at the time.'

He tightened his arms around her, pressing his forehead to hers as he grumbled, 'You see, if you'd just *said that at the time* then this wouldn't have taken anywhere near as long!'

She raised her long lashes and smiled a meaningful smile at him. 'And miss out on the cabin in the woods?'

'When you cried? That part I'd have skipped. I don't ever want you to cry because of me again. I thought I'd done something very wrong and it killed me. When what had happened—when there was nothing between our bodies—'

He almost choked on the words and Merrow loved him even more. 'It was just the most incredibly amazing...I mean...I've never...'

There was nothing in the world as beautiful to behold as a strong man made weak by the woman he loved, was there? And she'd done this to him. She was *his* weakness too.

She stopped unbuttoning and lifted her hands to his face, staring across into his gorgeous eyes to inform him in a firm voice, 'Why do you think I was crying? It was the same for me. It was overwhelming, it was intense, I've never in my entire life felt so close to someone or had someone do to my body what you do. I just needed time to process it all. And to do that I needed space—I've always been that way. When something affects me emotionally I have to run away and sort through it on my own before I can come and talk about it. It's one of my failings. One of the ones I'm aware of but don't make public, remember? But you pushed. It was the wrong time to push me, that's all... And then you were *leaving me*—'

'O'Connell, I was never leaving you. I may fight with you the odd time and you may do the occasional thing that makes me feel like strangling you, but I was never, *ever* leaving you. If you hadn't come to find me this time I'd have hated you for a while and felt like a bloody idiot. But eventually I'd have hunted you down again and started over. You have to know that.'

Merrow's face lit up, and she kissed him again, long and deep, before informing him, 'I do *now*.'

'I love you, O'Connell. I will 'til the day I die. And I'm up to the goldfish, which you already understand—so, *no more secrets*—and I'm ready for my *rewards*—'

She placed a finger on his mouth when he leaned in, squirming a little and unable to look him in the eye. 'Erm, one more secret…'

His eyebrows rose in question.

Merrow blushed when she looked at him. 'And this is a *secret* secret. One I haven't told anyone, not even any of the musketeers.'

His eyes widened in surprise.

She searched the air, tilted her head from side to side. So Alex lifted his hand and removed her finger from his lips. 'And now you're scaring me a little.'

She fixed her gaze on his and smiled before she took a deep breath and confessed her deepest-held secret.

'When I left you in Galway that time, I cried myself to sleep for a week solid. I never told a soul, because they'd have wanted to know why. And at the time I didn't know why…'

Alex's voice was thick with emotion, his hand smoothing over her back to reassure her he was there now, that he wasn't going anywhere. 'And you know now?'

'Yes, I know now.' She smiled a tremulous smile, her eyes glittering as she looked at him. 'I think I knew the first time

I looked in your eyes that I would love you one day. I don't know why I felt that way, Alex, but I did. I looked into your eyes and it was like I already knew you and that sleeping with you wasn't just some seedy one-night stand. It was the start of something important.'

She saw his throat convulse and she laughed a low, half-sobbing laugh. 'I know. It's dumb. But it felt like I'd walked away from something huge and taken the chance on never finding it again. I felt so-o-o empty and when I cried I really sobbed my guts out, until I was so exhausted I fell asleep. It was like a bloody bereavement, I swear. And how could I ever have explained to anyone why I felt like that?'

He frowned, his hands stilling on her back as he whispered with wonder in his voice and in his eyes, 'You're shaking.'

'I know.' She half laughed again. 'How pathetic is that? Even remembering how it felt does that to me.'

'Shh.' He kissed the memory away, then held her in his arms and rocked her, whispering how much he loved her into her ear until the shaking stopped and the inevitable heat began to rise between their bodies, and then he whispered, 'Let's go and make you feel better, shall we, O'Connell?'

'Now you're talking.' She lifted her legs and wrapped them around his hips, her arms around his neck as he lifted her off the counter and swung round to carry her down the hall, raining kisses on her neck along the way.

'You do know you won't be able to call me O'Connell any more when my name's Fitzgerald?'

'You'll always be my *O'Connell*.' He mumbled the words against her neck. 'Even when you're a Fitzgerald.'

Merrow leaned back, waiting for his head to rise and hazel to look into green before she grinned at him, her heart in her eyes. 'You know, that very thought scared me once, but now that I know you're *my Fitzgerald*—I'm fine with it. It's *perfect*. Just promise me something?'

'*Anything*. I love you.'

'I love you too. Just promise me we'll *elope*.'

* * * * *

Silhouette Desire kicks off 2009 with
MAN OF THE MONTH, *a yearlong program*
featuring incredible heroes by stellar authors.

When navy SEAL Hunter Cabot returns home for some
much-needed R & R, he discovers he's a married man.
There's just one problem: he's never met his "bride."

Enjoy this sneak peek at Maureen Child's
AN OFFICER AND A MILLIONAIRE.
Available January 2009 from Silhouette Desire.

One

Hunter Cabot, Navy SEAL, had a healing bullet wound in his side, thirty days' leave and, apparently, a wife he'd never met.

On the drive into his hometown of Springville, California, he stopped for gas at Charlie Evans's service station. That's where the trouble started.

"Hunter! Man, it's good to see you! Margie didn't tell us you were coming home."

"Margie?" Hunter leaned back against the front fender of his black pickup truck and winced as his side gave a small twinge of pain. Silently then, he watched as the man he'd known since high school filled his tank.

Charlie grinned, shook his head and pumped gas. "Guess your wife was lookin' for a little 'alone' time with you, huh?"

"My—" Hunter couldn't even say the word. *Wife?* He didn't have a wife. "Look, Charlie..."

"Don't blame her, of course," his friend said with a wink as he finished up and put the gas cap back on. "You being gone all the time with the SEALs must be hard on the ol' love life."

He'd never had any complaints, Hunter thought, frowning at the man still talking a mile a minute. "What're you—"

"Bet Margie's anxious to see you. She told us all about that

R and R trip you two took to Bali." Charlie's dark brown eyebrows lifted and wiggled.

"Charlie..."

"Hey, it's okay, you don't have to say a thing, man."

What the hell could he say? Hunter shook his head, paid for his gas and as he left, told himself Charlie was just losing it. Maybe the guy had been smelling gas fumes too long.

But as it turned out, it wasn't just Charlie. Stopped at a red light on Main Street, Hunter glanced out his window to smile at Mrs. Harker, his second-grade teacher who was now at least a hundred years old. In the middle of the crosswalk, the old lady stopped and shouted, "Hunter Cabot, you've got yourself a wonderful wife. I hope you appreciate her."

Scowling now, he only nodded at the old woman—the only teacher who'd ever scared the crap out of him. What the hell was going on here? Was everyone but him nuts?

His temper beginning to boil, he put up with a few more comments about his "wife" on the drive through town before finally pulling into the wide, circular drive leading to the Cabot mansion. Hunter didn't have a clue what was going on, but he planned to get to the bottom of it. Fast.

He grabbed his duffel bag, stalked into the house and paid no attention to the housekeeper, who ran at him, fluttering both hands. "Mr. Hunter!"

"Sorry, Sophie," he called out over his shoulder as he took the stairs two at a time. "Need a shower, then we'll talk."

He marched down the long, carpeted hallway to the rooms that were always kept ready for him. In his suite, Hunter tossed the duffel down and stopped dead. The shower in his bathroom was running. His *wife?*

Anger and curiosity boiled in his gut, creating a churning mass that had him moving forward without even thinking about it. He opened the bathroom door to a wall of steam and the sound of a woman singing—off-key. Margie, no doubt.

Well, if she was his wife...Hunter walked across the room, yanked the shower door open and stared in at a curvy, naked, temptingly wet woman.

She whirled to face him, slapping her arms across her naked body while she gave a short, terrified scream.

Hunter smiled. "Hi, honey. I'm home."

* * * * *

Be sure to look for
AN OFFICER AND A MILLIONAIRE
by USA TODAY *bestselling author Maureen Child.*
Available January 2009 from Silhouette Desire.

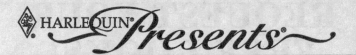

HARLEQUIN *Presents*

Demure but defiant...
Can three international playboys
tame their disobedient brides?

Lynne Graham

presents

THE GREEK TYCOON'S DISOBEDIENT BRIDE
Available December 2008, Book #2779

THE RUTHLESS MAGNATE'S VIRGIN MISTRESS
Available January 2009, Book #2787

THE SPANISH BILLIONAIRE'S PREGNANT WIFE
Available February 2009, Book #2795

www.eHarlequin.com
HP12787

REQUEST YOUR FREE BOOKS!

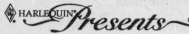

2 FREE NOVELS PLUS 2 FREE GIFTS!

PASSION GUARANTEED SEDUCTION

YES! Please send me 2 FREE Harlequin Presents® novels and my 2 FREE gifts (gifts are worth about $10). After receiving them, if I don't wish to receive any more books, I can return the shipping statement marked "cancel". If I don't cancel, I will receive 6 brand-new novels every month and be billed just $4.05 per book in the U.S. or $4.74 per book in Canada, plus 25¢ shipping and handling per book and applicable taxes, if any*. That's a savings of close to 15% off the cover price! I understand that accepting the 2 free books and gifts places me under no obligation to buy anything. I can always return a shipment and cancel at any time. Even if I never buy another book, the two free books and gifts are mine to keep forever.

106 HDN ERRW 306 HDN ERRL

Name	(PLEASE PRINT)
Address	Apt. #
City	State/Prov.	Zip/Postal Code

Signature (if under 18, a parent or guardian must sign)

Mail to the **Harlequin Reader Service:**
IN U.S.A.: P.O. Box 1867, Buffalo, NY 14240-1867
IN CANADA: P.O. Box 609, Fort Erie, Ontario L2A 5X3

Not valid to current subscribers of Harlequin Presents books.

Want to try two free books from another line?
Call 1-800-873-8635 or visit www.morefreebooks.com.

* Terms and prices subject to change without notice. N.Y. residents add applicable sales tax. Canadian residents will be charged applicable provincial taxes and GST. Offer not valid in Quebec. This offer is limited to one order per household. All orders subject to approval. Credit or debit balances in a customer's account(s) may be offset by any other outstanding balance owed by or to the customer. Please allow 4 to 6 weeks for delivery. Offer available while quantities last.

Your Privacy: Harlequin Books is committed to protecting your privacy. Our Privacy Policy is available online at www.eHarlequin.com or upon request from the Reader Service. From time to time we make our lists of customers available to reputable third parties who may have a product or service of interest to you. If you would prefer we not share your name and address, please check here. ☐

HP08R

HARLEQUIN Presents

MISTRESS
TO A
MILLIONAIRE

She's his in the bedroom, but he can't buy her love...

Showered with diamonds,
draped in exquisite lingerie,
whisked around the world...
The ultimate fantasy becomes a reality
in
Sharon Kendrick's

BOUGHT FOR THE SICILIAN BILLIONAIRE'S BED

Available Janary 2009
Book #2789

Live the dream with more
Mistress to a Millionaire titles
by your favorite authors

Coming soon!

HP12789